Gabe Maxfield remembers Manuel Delgado all too well—since investigating him nearly got him killed. He'd be very happy never to see him again, but that's not in the cards for him. When the mother of a missing socialite seeks out Paradise Investigations to find out what happened to her daughter, Gabe and best friend Grace Park are going to be thrown right back into Delgado's world. Personal lives begin to interfere, as well, and soon they've got more on their plate than they can handle.

A missing woman.

Delgado's son.

A romantically awkward Grace.

Gabe's parents.

It's just another week for Gabe Maxfield.

PALM TREES AND PAPARAZZI

Gabe Maxfield Mysteries, Book Three

J.C. Long

A NineStar Press Publication

Published by NineStar Press
P.O. Box 91792,
Albuquerque, New Mexico, 87199 USA.
www.ninestarpress.com

Palm Trees and Paparazzi

Printed in the USA
First Edition
July, 2018

Print ISBN: 978-1-951057-04-6

Also available in eBook, ISBN: 978-1-951057-03-9

Warning: This book contains sexually explicit content, which may only be suitable for mature readers.

Prologue

BELIEVE IT OR not—and most people won't—I never wanted to have a rip-roaring, exciting life. Some people might be thrill seekers, going out and free jumping or doing parkour or rock climbing without safety equipment, but I did not fall into that category, and I never did.

I was perfectly satisfied imagining a quiet, tranquil life, the occasional night out with my friends, a boring job taking pictures of cheating spouses—maybe something as exciting as finding long-lost birth parents—and quiet nights spent in the arms of my boyfriend. That was the image I had of the perfect life.

And yet, somehow, the adventure kept finding me, whether I liked it or not.

The missing daughter of a wealthy socialite.

The return of an old enemy.

Mystery men turning up every time I turned around.

The unwelcome arrival of my parents in Hawaii.

Yep, it looked like everything was just business as usual at Paradise Investigations.

Chapter One

THERE WAS A time when throbbing music, frenetically moving bodies, and expensive cocktails would have been my scene—a time that passed a few years back, I'd guess. Actually, you know what? Scratch that. I've never been one for clubs. And with my twenty-ninth birthday merely two months away, it was really time for me to close that chapter of my life, anyway.

It was the second week of January, and some people still hadn't lost the edge from New Year's Eve. The club was packed full of people even though it was a Wednesday—thanks, no doubt, to ladies' night and slightly discounted drinks for men.

My best friend, Grace Park, and I managed to snag a table that was far enough from the speakers that we wouldn't be deafened for days to come by the outing.

Grace sat at the table, stirring the thin black straw in her vodka tonic, which she'd barely had half of. I'd volunteered to drive us tonight so Grace could have a few drinks, and she hadn't finished her first one in the hour we'd been there.

"You look miserable, Grace," I said, nudging her with my shoulder. "If you want to go home, just say the word. Really, we don't need to stay here on my account."

"I'm fine, Gabe," she insisted stubbornly, even though I knew her well enough to know she wasn't. She'd been down ever since New Year's Eve. She'd been invited to a party by Jin Hamada, our private investigation firm's resident tech expert and object of Grace's affection, and had assumed it was a romantic invitation only to show up, dressed to the nines and ready, to discover it was a casual thing he threw for the people who lived in his apartment building. Jin hadn't noticed, but Grace had been mortified.

It didn't help that our assistant, Mrs. Neidermeyer, who lives in Jin's building, *did* notice and teased Grace about it every chance that she got.

Privately, I thought Grace was taking it a little hard, but who was I to judge? I literally fled the continent to escape a breakup. That didn't put me in the running for the category of most reasonable reaction to something.

"I thought coming to this club would cheer you up a little bit," I said, taking a sip of my ginger ale—no alcohol for me, since I was driving. "I hate seeing you so down. I know how much you love music and dancing and clubs."

Grace snorted. "When we were in college, yeah. But you know, maybe...maybe we're a little old for this crowd."

"I was just thinking the same thing," I admitted. "When did that happen, though? When did we get old?"

"Kind of sneaked up on us, didn't it? Here we are, just around the corner from thirty. Remember when we watched *Friends* in high school and we thought they were all overreacting about turning thirty? Now that we're looking it in the face, I'm starting to think maybe they weren't overreacting that much after all."

"It's not that bad," I said consolingly. It was a weird reversal for us; usually Grace was the one doing her best to make *me* feel better, not the other way around. "Think about how high life expectancy is? Nowadays people don't even really get started before they're thirty."

"Not so bad? Come on, Gabe. We're almost thirty and I'm still single. I *do* want to have kids someday, you know? That's getting more and more unlikely the longer I stay single." She picked up her vodka tonic, tossing it back as if she could wash away the dour thoughts with it.

At least she drank it; that cost me six dollars.

"Don't you think you're taking this whole thing too seriously Grace? So you made a mistake and misinterpreted his invitation. You think you're the first person to ever make that mistake?"

Grace scowled at my reminder. "I looked like an idiot."

"No one even noticed!"

"Mrs. Neidermeyer almost has an aneurism from laughing every time she sees me!"

"Okay, so no one but Mrs. Neidermeyer even noticed."

"That old lady is enough."

"I don't understand the rivalry you two have."

"She's got it out for me!"

"No, she doesn't. She's just spirited."

"She's medicated."

I decided to drop the Neidermeyer discussion. It was a sore spot for her, and one that wouldn't go away—particularly since I basically hired her to annoy Grace. The last thing I wanted to do then was to bring Grace down even more by talking about something that she hated.

I surveyed the bodies on the dance floor, taking in the sights, wondering if I could get a jolt of energy from them by proxy. Everyone seemed to be having so much fun, but then again that's what clubs were, right? There were no doubt a large number of tourists among the crowd, people itching to get away from the tourist elements of Honolulu and into something that they were familiar with. Sure, the locale might be different, but a club was a club, whether it was in Seattle, New York, Pontiac, Michigan, or Honolulu.

"We've got company," Grace said, drawing my attention from the crowd. I spotted my boyfriend, Maka Kekoa, making his way toward us around the perimeter of the room. A wide smile stretched my lips when I saw him. He was tall, his skin a sun-kissed brown that proudly displayed his Native Hawaiian heritage. His body was lean, hard muscle, kept that way by his rigorous exercise routine, his frequent surfing, and his job on the police force.

Walking behind Maka but still casting a shadow over him was one of Maka's best friends, Hiapo, a big guy with an even bigger heart who ran an exclusive and popular lu'au on the island. Hiapo was without a doubt one of the cheeriest people I had ever met.

"Yo, howzit?" Hiapo greeted, his naturally loud voice easy to hear over the drone of techno dance music blaring in the background, a remix of a remix of a Cher song, if I had to guess.

"Hey, guys," I greeted, moving my seat a little so Maka could make room on the other side of the table for himself and Hiapo.

Maka smiled at me, a look that always somehow managed to look sultry and goofy at the same time.

"Hey." He planted a gentle, chaste kiss on my lips.

Beside me, Grace made a strange sound, a cross between a *harrumph* and a *tsk*. Maka cast an amused look her way. "I see your plan to cheer her up is right on schedule."

"I don't need cheering up," Grace huffed.

"Girl, you still pining over that IT guy?" Hiapo asked.

"No," Grace said at the same time Maka and I said, "Yes!" earning us both glowers.

"Traitors."

"Listen, you need me to put something together for you? Plan a nice romantic package, like I did for these two here?" He indicated Maka and I with a thumb.

"I appreciate the offer, Hiapo, but that won't be necessary. I don't even think he likes me."

"Have you asked him out?"

Grace squirmed in her seat. "No. But we've known each other for three years, and he's never asked me out in all of this time. I think if he was interested, he would have done something about it already, right?"

"I see one major flaw in that logic, Gracie," I said. "You like him, but you haven't done anything about it, either."

Grace's brow furrowed as she struggled to come up with a comeback, but I could see in her eyes that she couldn't. "I just don't want to waste any more time on someone who might not even like me back. That's time I could better spend going out with people who are interested."

"But who you're not interested in," I added.

Grace threw her hands up in the air. "Is this beat up Grace night? Are you trying to cheer me up by making me more depressed?"

"Okay, okay, you win. I'll stop."

We stayed there for another hour, doing our best to get Grace to cheer up with very limited success. Finally we decided to call it a night. Maka and Hiapo left together, and I took Grace home.

We rode without talking, listening to various covers of songs by the Dynamos. As crazy as it might sound, I hate the Dynamos but really enjoy the songs themselves. I just can't stand hearing *them* do the singing.

Finally I couldn't take it anymore, and just before reaching the neighborhood she lived in I asked, "Are you really going to give up on Jin?"

Grace heaved a sigh, looking out the window, hand propped up under her chin, elbow on the door. With her sitting like that, I could imagine Grace being in a movie, with a deep, soulful soundtrack—maybe something by Adele—playing in the background.

"Don't you think I should? It seems clear to me that he isn't interested."

"It's not clear to me," I said, pulling my car to a stop in front of Grace's place. "Not until you ask him."

"I'm not going to just waltz up to him and ask him! Don't be ridiculous." Grace unbuckled her seatbelt and pushed open the car door.

I shrugged nonchalantly. "Okay, then, fine. Let Mrs. Neidermeyer win."

She took the bait, just like I knew she would, stopping halfway out of the car and fixing a stern glare on me. "What is that supposed to mean?"

"You're always saying that she's against you and doesn't want you seeing Jin," I reminded her. I hoped that the best way to build up her confidence was to give her an enemy that wasn't herself. I didn't feel too badly about it, considering she pretty much disliked Mrs. Neidermeyer the moment she set eyes on her. "If you just give up without really knowing, all you're doing is giving her exactly what she wants, right?"

"I'll think about it," Grace said after considering my words. "I'll see you at work tomorrow."

"Goodnight, Grace." I sat in front of her place until she was safely inside before driving home. I really hoped Grace did think about what I said and finally took the leap and asked Jin—that or move on, because working with her in this sort of funk was beginning to get a little tiring.

And, if I was being completely honest, it felt really juvenile, like high school all over again. I was ready for Grace to go back to her normal self. Maybe that made me a bad friend, but I looked at it a different way. Grace pushed me to get out of the condo and out into the world of the living once more after I arrived in Hawai'i, and I was returning the favor now.

I only hoped she would appreciate it as much as I did.

WHEN I SHOWED up to work the next morning, I was surprised to find a shiny black limousine sitting in the parking lot, taking up what few parking spots actually existed outside of the office of Paradise Investigations where Grace and I worked as private investigators. Okay, technically Grace was the only one of us licensed, but I was working on it and hoped to have gotten it by the end of June.

Grace wasn't there yet, I saw, but Mrs. Neidermeyer was. I would know the lime-green 1979 Ford Pinto she drove anywhere. It had to be the only one left on the island—probably on any of the islands. Even if it had been a less recognizable car, the bright, sparkly pink window decal that said "Sexy Grandma" was a dead giveaway.

I eased my car into the spot beside the Pinto and got out. I tried to act casual and not attempt to peer through the dark tint of the limousine's windows to see who was inside. Maybe the driver was new and was looking up directions on his or her phone, or perhaps whoever was behind the wheel thought this place was abandoned and decided to pull in to grab a quick cat nap at eight-fifty in the morning.

Mrs. Neidermeyer sat behind her desk in the front lobby of the office when I entered. Today she'd chosen to wear a pair of far too skinny designer jeans and a white halter top that did nothing to hide the bright pink bra she wore under it. It was all thrown horribly off-kilter by the blue rinse in her curly hair.

"Good morning, Gabe," she greeted me brightly. "See the *schnazzy* limo outside?"

"Hard to miss. Like your outfit."

Mrs. Neidermeyer straightened in her chair, preening a bit. "You like it?"

"Come on, Mrs. Neidermeyer, you know you're only wearing that because Grace told you that sort of outfit is inappropriate for the workplace. You just want to mess with her head."

"That's not true! I also want to look good."

It was all I could do not to slap myself in the forehead. I'd brought this on myself, hiring her to annoy Grace. I hadn't considered the consequences, that I might get caught in the middle. The whole thing had been a poorly thought through mess. The only thing that kept me from bringing an end to it all was the fact that she was an old lady who desperately needed the job to support her incredibly awful spending habits.

Far be it for me to come between an elderly woman and her Gucci.

"What's with the limo out—oh good lord, Mrs. Neidermeyer!"

That would be Grace. I looked over my shoulder to see her standing there in the doorway, a look of disgust plain on her face.

Don't react, I mouthed to her desperately. Grace was a smart woman; she knew that Mrs. Neidermeyer just wanted to provoke a reaction from her, she knew it and yet she still insisted on walking into the trap knowing full well it was a trap. The irrationality of it baffled me.

"That is *way* too much skin to be showing in the work place!"

Mrs. Neidermeyer let out a short, sharp cackle. "I'd like to see you pull something like this off!"

Grace stalked toward Mrs. Neidermeyer's desk, getting geared up for a full-fledged battle. "I'd like to pull that off of you and burn it!"

"Guys," I said patiently, trying to be the voice of reason. "Can I just remind you that there's a limousine with an unknown passenger parked out front? And we don't have curtains on the windows."

Grace took a deep calming breath, much to my relief. "You know what? You're right. It's not worth it. What do I care if she makes a fool of herself in public?"

"Jealousy," Mrs. Neidermeyer said in a singsong voice. "It must be hard going through life that envious, Grace."

"It must be hard going through life without taking your medication," Grace shot back.

Outside a car door shut. "Enough," I said firmly, giving them both my best *I mean it* glare. The last thing Paradise Investigations needed was a public squabble. We were still having a hard time establishing a reputation for ourselves, even though we'd been involved in two majorly high-profile cases. Well, only one if you didn't count the murder of Grace's former business partner, Carrie. Back in September we'd helped uncover a hidden tontine containing a wealth of artwork stolen from the Japanese in the Pacific during World War Two. Since then, though, we'd sort of fizzled right back into this purgatory of sorts. We still got a few cases a month, but none of it was enough to justify all of our expenses.

A limousine outside might be the answer to our financial prayers, if I could keep these two from killing each other long enough to give a somewhat decent impression to whoever was in it.

"*If* this is a potential customer, the last thing we want to do is scare them off, right? We need the money. I don't know how much longer we can stay in business the way things are going. So *be professional!*"

"Be professional?" Grace repeated incredulously. "It won't matter *how* professional we are with Mrs. Neidermeyer sitting here in *that!*"

The last thing I wanted to do was get caught in the middle of them, but Grace had a point. We would have a hard time being taken seriously if Mrs. Neidermeyer and her...interesting...clothing style was the first thing they saw. There was nothing we could do about that right now, but I was determined to have a talk with her about her fashion choices in the near future.

A second car door closed outside and then there was a uniformed chauffeur opening the door. The woman who came through the door was beautiful, elegant, and dressed in clothing that probably cost as much as our monthly rent for the office. Her features were strong, her brown eyes like stone and yet somehow emotionally vulnerable at the same time. Her sleek black hair was pulled back into a long ponytail that reached down to the small of her back.

"Welcome to Paradise Investigations," Grace said with a winning smile, stepping over so she was in front of Mrs. Neidermeyer's desk. "I'm Grace Park, this is my partner, Gabe Maxfield."

I nodded politely at my name.

"I'm Helena Hu," she introduced herself briskly. She had the voice of a woman who stood in her power, confident and always in control. I found myself admiring her instantly, just from those three words. "I'm here to seek your services. I apologize if it seems forward, but considering the nature of my request and the fact that time is of the essence, I'd like to get straight to it, if you don't mind."

"Uh, well, of course," I said, shooting a glance at Grace. "Why don't you follow us? We can speak in my office."

I led the way through the door that opened back into what used to be the three examination rooms of the dentist office before we bought it and turned it into our own. Once through the door I motioned for Helena to take one of the two seats across from my desk. Grace stood next to me as I sat down in my chair.

"What is it you'd like us to do for you, Mrs. Hu?"

"I want you to find my daughter," she said immediately.

It wasn't what I expected. I assumed she wanted us to track a cheating spouse or find a way to get around a prenuptial agreement or something equally *Dallas*-esque. Finding someone? That was new territory.

"Do you mean that you want us to find someone you put up for adoption?"

"No. My daughter, Christine Hu, is missing. She has been for three days. I want you to find out where she is."

"Uh, Mrs. Hu," Grace said carefully, brow furrowed. "No offense intended, but this sounds like it's something the police should be handling, not private detectives."

Helena tutted. "The police are convinced she ran off with her personal assistant."

I raised an eyebrow. "Well, did she?"

"Absolutely not," Helena replied crossly. "That's not the kind of person my daughter is. I know how it can seem—she's a Honolulu socialite, grew up in money, always in the paper, but she's no Lindsey Lohan or Paris Hilton. My daughter is a serious woman who loves her family. Her father died when she was seventeen, so I'm all the family she has. We're very close. She would never just run off and leave me. Besides, she's engaged. She wouldn't have thrown that away for some fling with her personal assistant."

"What makes the police so certain that's what happened?" Grace asked, picking up a notepad and a pen from my desk and jotting down some preliminary notes.

"Because Travis—that's the personal assistant, Travis Brent—disappeared the same day."

I didn't say it, but it sounded to me like perhaps Helena Hu didn't know her daughter as well as she might. That wasn't really a judgment for me to make, though, having never seen them interact together and not knowing the personal details of their lives. My first instinct was to say that money always screwed up families—my family being a prime example—but I reminded myself that my family wasn't really representative of all people with money.

If Helena said her daughter wouldn't do that, then I had to trust her judgment on the matter.

"Is there anything you can tell us about your daughter that might be relevant? Any places she likes to go, establishments she frequents? You mentioned a fiancé?"

Helena reached into her Coach purse and took out a piece of paper. "Here's a list of all of the places she usually goes to. You won't find a lot of nightlife spots on the list; it wasn't her thing. And yes, she recently got engaged. Last month, actually. The announcement was really big news." A second piece of paper followed the first, this one a folded-up newspaper clipping.

"'Socialite daughter of Honolulu philanthropist set to marry in the fall,'" Grace read. Under the headline was a photo of a couple. The woman was without a doubt Helena's daughter, Christine. She was the spitting image of her mother. She had a brilliant smile that managed to shine through even in the black and white photo.

The man next to her was handsome in a roguish sort of way, with a narrow chin, high cheekbones, and a large nose that looked like it had suffered many breaks throughout his life. Something in his face was recognizable.

They both looked happy next to each other, a couple in love from what I could see.

"They look happy," Grace said, mirroring my thoughts.

"They do," Helena agreed. "Although I have my own misgivings about the two of them."

"Why is that?" Grace asked.

"Oh, I think I know," I said before Helena could speak. I reread the caption beneath the picture three times, and each time the knot in my stomach grew tighter. "'Pictured: Christine Hu and fiancé Sergio Delgado photographed at the announcement of their engagement.'" I looked up at Helena. "Delgado, as in Manuel Delgado?"

"Yes. Sergio is his eldest son."

"Well," I said, letting that sink in, "I guess I can understand the misgivings. Then again, you probably already guessed that, right?"

Helena smiled a little bit. "That's true enough. I sought you out because I know of your past dealings with the Delgado family. You two are among the minuscule list of people I can trust aren't in Manuel Delgado's pocket."

"You can say that again," Grace growled. We both knew without any doubt that Manuel Delgado was the man behind the death of Grace's former business partner, but we couldn't prove it. He was a rich and influential man on the island, and had the power to protect himself.

Helena arched an eyebrow. "So, I take it you're going to take the job?"

I tilted my head toward Grace, who gave me a nod. "Mrs. Hu, you've got yourself private investigators."

Chapter Two

IT DIDN'T TAKE more than twenty minutes to settle on a decent contract. Helena agreed immediately to our normal fee and the terms of exactly what it was she was wanting us to do. She provided us with all the details we needed to get underway and gave us her cell phone number so we could provide her with updates when we felt it necessary.

Grace and I stood there, side by side, watching the limousine drive away.

"So," Grace said when it was out of sight. "Are you ready to tangle with Delgado again?"

"Yes." And I was, I really was. Of course I hoped he had nothing to do with Christine, and that the rumor about her running off with someone else turned out to be true. However, knowing what I knew about that man's ruthlessness, I wouldn't be surprised if Helena was right. It definitely required closer investigation.

"Well, we can't just march up to his office and accuse him of yet another crime," Grace said, turning on her heel and heading back inside our office. "We've got to lay the groundwork. The information Mrs. Hu gave us is great, but we need to know a little more. What did she say was the name of the lead investigator from missing persons?"

"'Ōpūnui, I think," I answered.

"That's where we should start, then. Mrs. Neidermeyer, could you call Honolulu Police and let a Detective 'Ōpūnui know that we are coming?"

Mrs. Neidermeyer heaved a put-upon sigh. "I guess."

"Good," Grace said, grabbing her car keys. "And while we're gone, go change your clothes."

"That's not going to happen."

Grace rolled her eyes at me as we exited the office once more, making for her car. "I knew it was a long shot, but I had to try."

"I'll have a talk with her," I assured Grace as we got in the car and buckled up.

"Someone needs to," Grace grumbled. "I'm trying not to imagine how many potential clients might have been scared away by her ridiculous clothing."

"I'm sure it's not that many," I assured her, though I was in fact not sure at all. There was no way we'd ever know, but I'd guess it had happened on at least a few occasions. It was a good thing for us we didn't get too many walk-ins. Most of our business came from telephone or website appointments. People assumed we were busier than we actually were.

Grace drove us, still not trusting my legendarily bad navigation skills. I couldn't fault her for that, because it was true. I wasn't good at navigating around even in a city I knew well, and though I'd been in Honolulu for several months, I still wasn't comfortable with it. The police station, though, that was a place I could get to in my sleep, since Maka worked there.

"Do you think this detective is going to tell us anything?" I asked as we arrived at HPD. "I thought they didn't comment on on-going investigations."

Grace scoffed. "We're not reporters. I can usually get HPD to tell me *something* at least." She cast a wry look my way. "And we both know how effective you are with getting police officers to do what you want."

I had no response to that other than to glare. There was no way in hell I was going to put the moves on any of the missing persons detectives, even to get information. I didn't think Maka would like it anyway.

"Maybe you should let me do the talking," Grace suggested. "Since I've got experience at this, I mean. Not that I don't think you can do it."

I rolled my eyes. "Oh, show me your ways, *sensei*."

According to the board near the entrance, missing persons was located on the third floor of the building. Missing Persons was one of those departments with a big budget, like Homicide, and they had the whole floor to themselves by the looks of it.

We took the stairs up—Grace had a thing about elevators—and almost as soon as we left the stairwell onto the floor, we were approached by a pretty detective in a suit, her badge visible on her belt.

"Can I help you?"

"We're looking for Detective ʻŌpūnui," Grace said. "Can you point him out to us?"

The woman frowned a little bit, like she was wondering what we wanted with him, and then pointed toward an older man in a pinstriped suit, the jacket thrown casually over his chair, about halfway along the bullpen. His face was weathered from a life in the sun, his hairline receding ever so slightly, like it had started and then he'd stopped it by sheer force of will.

If I was being honest with myself, just looking at him made me feel intimidated. It didn't make much sense; he wasn't the most imposing man, and I'd long since gotten used to being around physically big men, with Maka and Hiapo and some of Maka's other friends.

Detective 'Ōpūnui had something different though, something even Maka lacked most of the time we were together, and that was an aura— this halo of intimidation as bright as the Northern Lights.

Grace started forward without me and then gestured for me to catch up when she realized I was still standing in place. I reluctantly followed behind her, steeling myself for the inevitable.

"Detective 'Ōpūnui?" Grace asked politely as she approached the desk. The desk's name plaque read "Richard 'Ōpūnui." I noticed her voice had altered slightly, dipping down into a lower register, the way it did when she was intent on charming someone.

For his part, the detective didn't much look like he wanted to be charmed. He looked between Grace and me for a moment before he grunted.

"I don't talk to reporters."

"Oh, we're not reporters. I'm Grace Park, and this is my apprentice, Gabe Maxfield."

I wanted to kick her in that moment; I *hated* when she introduced me as her apprentice, though I technically was. It made it sound like I was some know-nothing kid following her around on career day.

"We're private investigators."

'Ōpūnui snorted then. "The two of you?"

I saw a flash of irritation burst through Grace's professional shell before she repressed it. "Yes. Paradise Investigations. Maybe you've heard of us?"

"Isn't Kekoa from Homicide banging one of you?"

I fought to keep from blushing. Normally it would be a losing battle, but I'd finally picked up a tan in Hawai'i, thank god.

"I really don't think that's relevant."

I regretted speaking the moment the words ended, because ʻŌpūnui turned his sharp gaze on me and gave a nod, as if he'd answered some internal question.

"Kekoa always did have a thing for *haole*. Look, I don't make it a habit of talking to wannabe cops, either."

"This won't take long," Grace said, plopping down in one of the two uncomfortable chairs across from ʻŌpūnui's desk. "We just wanted to ask you a few questions about the Christine Hu case."

At the mention of Christine Hu's name, it was as if a door slammed shut behind ʻŌpūnui's eyes. His entire bearing changed: he straightened in his seat and his hands clenched. The uneasy feeling I already had worsened.

"It's department policy not to comment on ongoing investigations, Ms. Park."

"We were hired by the missing woman's mother, Helena Hu. She wants to make sure the truth behind what happened to her daughter is reached as soon as possible."

It didn't take a rocket scientist to know Grace could have worded that better. I flinched inwardly as I heard it. If it sounded that way to me, I could only imagine how it would come across to ʻŌpūnui.

"Are you implying that HPD can't do its job, Ms. Park?"

There it goes, I thought with a grimace.

"What?" Grace blinked rapidly and began backpedaling. "No, of course not. What I meant was simply that Mrs. Hu is invested in this case—"

"And we're not?" ʻŌpūnui challenged. "Listen carefully: I've dealt with people like Helena Hu before. They're wealthy, and they throw their money around. She's hired you because she thinks the conclusion HPD is heading toward is one she doesn't like. Civilians shouldn't go around messing with police investigations. Yeah, you've gotten away with it before—" This he aimed directly at me. "—but it's not something you should make a habit of doing."

"We don't want to mess with your investigation," Grace said, her voice returning to its normal octave. "What we want is to make sure the truth is discovered. We don't want to see Christine Hu become another one of those people who just disappear without any answers, for her mother's sake."

'Ōpūnui looked around, rolling his eyes and pointing in our direction like he was asking if anyone else around was listening to us. "I've got some advice for you, Ms. Park, Mr. Maxfield: remember that you aren't cops. Stick to videoing guys banging their secretaries or finding lost poodles. Leave real police work to real police."

"Thank you for your time, Detective," I said, putting a hand on Grace's arm before she could spit out one of her usual retorts. I rose, forcing her up with me, and practically had to shove her to the stairs.

"Can you *believe* him?" she hissed once we were out of earshot. "I mean, really, can you believe him?"

"Considering you implied he couldn't do his job correctly, yes," I said, deadpan. "Speaking of which, *that* was your so-called rapport with the police? Can I guess that Carrie was the one who handled them?"

Grace looked down her nose at me. "I'm better with uniformed patrolmen."

"Uh huh." We started making our way down the stairs. "This might be a record for us, Gracie. Running into a wall an hour after taking a case? Impressive."

"We didn't hit a wall," Grace argued, leading the way down the stairs. "We hit a speed bump. If the missing persons detective won't tell us what we need to know, we have to find another angle." She looked at me expectantly.

"What do you—oh, I get it." She wanted me to use my relationship with Maka to get information. "Listen, Grace, I don't know how comfortable I am using the fact that Maka is my boyfriend to get information on a police investigation. I feel like that's putting him in an awkward place."

Grace stopped on the stairs and turned a pouty look my way. "What's the point of you having a cop boyfriend if we're not going to benefit from it?"

"Hey, I benefit from it in a *lot* of ways!"

Grace made a face. "Gross. Can we at least give him the chance to turn us down?"

I sighed. "Fine. We'll have better luck if we come around lunch time. And bring food. We're getting nowhere without food."

WE KILLED TIME driving to get lunch for Maka—Teddy's Bigger Burgers, the only fast-food place Maka really enjoyed. He'd introduced it to me, insisting it would change my world, and I had to admit, it did. Best burgers I'd ever eaten, bar none.

"I hope this works," Grace grumbled as the smell of delicious burgers filled the car. "That place is expensive."

"What do you care? We're charging it to Helena Hu anyway."

"Well, it *is* a business expense."

When we pulled back into the precinct parking lot, I turned to Grace. "I'm not going to pressure him. If he doesn't tell us anything, that's fine. We'll just have to find some other angle."

Grace put a hand to her chest like she was offended. "I wouldn't put you in that position! Okay, I would, but now that you've made it perfectly clear I wouldn't dream of it."

That settled, we headed inside. Heads turned our way as we walked through the precinct with our bags laden with salty, greasy food. I couldn't blame any of them, and I suspected we'd influenced at least one or two detective's lunch choices for the day.

Maka looked up at our approach and a wide grin spread across his handsome face. I couldn't help but smile in return; it was infectious. "Is that what I think it is?"

I held the bag up higher so he could see the logo on it, and he pressed his hands together as if he were saying a prayer of thanks.

Maka made room on the surface of his desk, pushing a lot of the paperwork and folders on it over to the desk of his partner, Detective Benet.

Thankfully Benet was nowhere to be seen. "Your partner not in today?" I tried to keep the hopefulness out of my voice as I unpacked the grease-stained bag.

"He went out to lunch. He just left, don't worry," Maka added, seeing my face. "If we eat quickly, you won't even see him."

"Thank god," Grace muttered, taking a sip of her Diet Coke.

"I don't see why you don't like him."

"Maybe it has something to do with the fact that he *arrested me for murder*?" Grace retorted.

"I was there, too."

Grace thought about that long enough to pop a thick-cut fry into her mouth. "Yes, but you weren't an asshole about it like he was."

"She's got you there." I unwrapped my hamburger and took a big bite, savoring the crunch of lettuce and tomato, the tangy bite of sharp cheddar cheese and the perfectly seasoned hamburger patty. Grace wasn't the only one who disliked Benet; there was a mutual antipathy between us that had existed from the first time we met, and I didn't see it going away anytime soon.

Luckily, it didn't appear that Maka had more than a functioning working relationship with him. In all the time I'd known him, he'd never invited Benet to his place or gone out drinking with him.

"Let's just eat, okay? No need to talk about Benet." Maka dug into his burger, consuming what looked like half of it in one bite.

"Actually, there's something we wanted to ask you." Grace futilely attempted to clean her greasy fingers on a napkin. "We accepted a job this morning. A woman wanting us to find her daughter who's gone missing. She says the general consensus seems to be that her daughter ran off with some guy, but the mother doesn't believe that."

Maka nodded, face guarded. "The Hu case, right? I've heard a few things about it."

"We went to talk to the detective in charge of the case, Detective 'Ōpūnui, but didn't get as much as we wanted."

"By that, she means we got nowhere," I clarified. "Even with her legendary ways with the police force."

Maka nodded knowingly. "'Ōpūnui can be a bit of a hard-ass, even with the other detectives in his own unit. I'm not surprised you didn't have much luck with him. What do you know about the case?"

"Christine Hu is the wealthy daughter of a local philanthropist. Recently engaged to Sergei Delgado. Yes," I added before Maka could speak, "*that* Delgado. Now you can understand why the mother isn't quick to buy the official line."

"Yeah, I can. You want me to see if I can get any other details for you from the investigation?"

"I don't want to put you in an awkward spot," I said quickly. "You're free to say no, if you want to."

Maka shrugged. "I don't think it's that big a deal. Considering the high-profile people in the case, the info is going to end up on the news eventually. You going to finish your fries?"

I wanted to say yes, but since Maka was helping us with this investigation I decided to be giving and nodded the go ahead. He scooped up what remained of my fries and popped several of them into his mouth.

I finished my burger, letting its wonderfulness settle in my stomach, warmth spreading through me. I was at my happiest after a good meal.

"By the way," Maka said as we were all crumpling up our burger wrappers and stuffing them into the bags, careful not to make a mess on the desk. "I was thinking, we should have a dinner party."

I raised an eyebrow. "A dinner party?"

"Yeah. It's a good chance to get together, you know. We can do it at my place. I'll make *poke.*"

What is he up to? In the entire time I'd known him, Maka hadn't struck me to be the dinner party type. Sure, we had the occasional dinners at his family's place, but he didn't do the cooking or host, and we could leave when the presence of others became too much to deal with.

"Considering how much you work with Jin, you should invite him, too," Maka said, as if it was an afterthought, though I knew better. Now I understood what he was doing.

"Jin?" Grace repeated, and her tone made it clear she saw Maka's intention as well. "Come on, guys, do you really think this is going to work? I've already messed up every other time I've tried."

"So you're just going to give up? I thought you liked him!"

Grace shifted her weight from foot to foot. "I do, but, I mean, there's only so many times a girl can fail before she has to stop, right?"

I patted her shoulder. "Come on, Grace, that's ridiculous. You're just letting yourself get too in your head. Maybe a laid-back environment would help you loosen up and stop being such a weirdo."

"Yeah, you know what, you're right. Maybe a dinner party isn't a bad idea. It's been a long time since I had good *poke.* When did you want to do this?"

Maka bit his lower lip, considering. "What about Saturday?"

"That's only two days away," I pointed out. "Think he doesn't already have plans?"

"Well, ask him and if he does, we'll reschedule for a time that works for him." Maka checked his watch. "I'm not saying that you need to leave, 'cause I love having you here, but Benet should be back from lunch soon."

Grace stood up immediately. "Well that's our cue to get the hell out of here."

I started to gather up the bags, but Maka stopped me. "Don't worry about it, I'll throw it away here." He stood and walked Grace and I down to the front door.

Grace gave the two of us a look and headed out first. Once she was gone, I smiled sheepishly at Maka. I still hadn't quite gotten used to the way Maka treated me, considering my last and only real adult relationship was with a guy who was with me for my money and emptied my bank account before running off. Trevor hadn't even wanted to hold hands in public.

Maka had no such qualms; right there where everyone could see, he leaned forward and kissed me gently on the lips. "See you later for movie night at your place?"

"Sounds good. I better go before Benet comes back. Wouldn't want to spoil what's turning out to be a pretty good day so far."

Maka couldn't quite hide his laugh, though he tried. "Okay. I'll call you when I finish work."

Maka left me there then to return to his desk, and I went out the door, a big smile on my face. Sure, Grace and I had just agreed to undertake what looked like it would end up being a difficult case, but it was a sunny day—well, a lot of the days were sunny, but still—and I had a great boyfriend. I had a hard time imagining anything bringing my spirits down today.

And then my phone rang.

It was a private number, and I didn't make it a habit of answering those. Everyone knew that answering blocked numbers could only end badly. I couldn't say what made me answer it that time. My only theory was that the giddiness I was feeling from the time spent with Maka had gone to my head and made me temporarily insane.

"Hello?" Silence greeted me, and I wondered if I'd gotten autodialed by a computer telemarketer; it sometimes takes a moment for their recorded message to kick in, since the company wanted to make sure that no part of it was cut off. "Hello?"

When the caller finally spoke, it was a woman's voice, and there was something about it that was familiar. For some reason the caller sounded very nervous. "Uh, yes, hello. This is, uh, this is Gabe Maxfield, right?"

"Yes," I answered carefully, waiting for the pitch to come.

"Gabriel? It's me."

My heart dropped twenty stories at my name. No one, I mean *no one*, had called me by my first name since I left home. All of a sudden, the reason for her voice sounding so familiar struck me.

"Mother?"

"Mother?" I repeated, wondering if I'd somehow fallen asleep and not realized it. There had to be some mistake. There was no way my mother was on the other end of that call. No way in hell.

The history of people using me went back further than Trevor. My parents wanted the perfect son, and when my grandfather left his money to me rather than them, they wanted the money from me, shamed me when I wouldn't give it to them. I'd left after high school and not once had I been back to see them since graduation day.

It couldn't possibly be her on the phone right then.

"Yes, Gabriel, it's me," she said, sounding choked up, which surprised me. My mother had never been the emotional sort, and certainly never in front of me. "I can't believe it's actually you."

"Trust me, the feeling is mutual," I said, mind reeling. I glanced toward Grace's car to catch her attention. At first, she waved me forward impatiently, but something on my face must have communicated the complex situation I was in, because the impatient look melted into a frown of concern.

"Hawaii is pretty far to go to run away from your parents."

Her words were like a bucket of icy water thrown over me. "How did you—how did you know I was in Hawai'i?"

"We saw a news story back in September," she answered. "Something about stolen Japanese art, and there you were on the screen. We hadn't known you'd moved; we thought you were still in San Francisco."

"I was never in San Francisco," I said irritably. "It was Seattle."

"Oh, of course, how silly of me. Anyway, we saw you and it made us realize how badly we wanted to talk to you again, how much we missed you. We hired a private detective to track you down, and well, here we are."

A car door closing caught my attention, and I saw Grace walking toward me.

"What do you want?" I asked, eager to bring the conversation to a close. Just talking to her made me feel like a teenager again and not a twenty-eight-year-old man.

"Well, your father and I are in Honolulu right now," she said.

"You're *here*?" I cried as Grace came to stand next to me. "You and Dad are here in Honolulu right now?" At the mention of my father Grace's eyes nearly bugged out of her head.

"Yes. We came all this way to find you. We want to see you."

What the hell was going on? Had I walked into an episode of *the Twilight Zone* or something? How was it that my parents were coming out of the woodwork now, after ten years? How had this day taken such a strange turn so quickly?

"That's not going to happen," I said, annoyed by the way my voice shook.

"Please, Gabriel," Mother pleaded, but she had to have known she wasn't going to get an answer that she liked when she'd asked the question. She couldn't have possibly expected me to agree to meet them.

"It's Gabe. And no, there's no way I'm going to meet you. I don't have anything to say to you."

"Did you ever think that maybe we had something we wanted to say to *you*?" There it was, for the first time since I'd answered the phone, a spark of the mother I knew so well. Fierce, domineering, far more interested in getting her own way than listening to what someone else wanted.

"I'm not interested in hearing anything you or Dad have to say, Mother."

I hung the phone up, unable to handle any more of the conversation. I stood there for a moment to gather my composure; I hadn't realized until just then that I was trembling.

"So that was—"

"Yes," I said tersely before she could mention my parents. "They hired a private investigator to track me down. Ironic, I guess. Anyway, let's just get back to work."

"Are you sure you don't want to talk about this?"

"Yes, Grace," I said firmly. "I'm very sure. Now can we please focus on the Christine Hu case? *Please*?"

Grace nodded. I was lucky and grateful that she could read me so well, see just how important it was to me that we let this go. "Of course. Come on, let's get back to work."

Chapter Three

WE SAT IN the parking lot debating what the next step was. It was hard for me to focus; the fact that my parents were currently on the island wouldn't leave my mind.

Why were my parents surfacing now, after all this time? As far as I knew they'd never attempted to find me before; they certainly hadn't made contact. Then again, I'd done my best to make sure of that—changing my number, not even telling them which of the universities I'd been accepted to I'd actually attend. I didn't *want* to hear from them.

"Gabe? Hello? I said what do you think?" Grace waved her hand in front of my face. She looked at me expectantly, awaiting my answer.

"What do I think about what?" At her exasperated sigh I felt compelled to apologize. "Sorry. I'm not in the right headspace right now."

"I can understand why, but this is important, so try to focus, okay?"

I nodded, doing my best to push thoughts of my parents out of my head. "Okay, okay, I'm focusing."

"I said that I think we have to try to talk to Sergio Delgado. He *is* the missing woman's fiancé, after all, so we'll have to talk to him eventually. I think. It's best to do it sooner rather than later."

As much as I didn't want to tangle with the Delgado family again, I could see the virtue in what Grace said. "Yeah. The longer we take, the more likely it is word will reach them that we're looking into the case. It's better to catch them off guard and hope that they slip up because they aren't expecting it."

Grace started her car now that we'd made a decision about our destination, a determined look on her face. "So, off we go into the belly of the beast." I wondered how much of that determination was bravado intended to mask her nervousness.

It made sense for her to be uneasy; Manuel Delgado was the man we both suspected of being behind the killing of her old partner as well as attempting to kill me when I looked into the murder. Grace had been in jail, charged with killing Carrie, while I'd conducted the investigation, so she'd never had any direct dealings with Delgado and only knew him by reputation. I could see how she might find him intimidating.

Hell, I still found him intimidating. It was hard not to, considering the power the man wielded, and the obvious ruthlessness he'd demonstrated. How much more severe would that be?

I did my best to keep my thoughts from drifting back to my personal issues. I needed all of my wits about me for what we were getting into.

We arrived at Delgado's office building, a modern glass structure that rose into the sky, sunlight gleaming off of it, so bright you needed to look away. The effect was harnessed perfectly. Delgado knew all about image and exactly how to use it to make people see what it was he wanted them to see and nothing else.

"There's a chance we won't even make it up to see him," I cautioned Grace as we stepped out of the car. "I only got in before because I was with Maka. I doubt Delgado will be so accommodating of us without a badge being flashed in his face."

We stepped inside, the temperature different enough that if I'd been wearing glasses, they would have fogged up instantly. I shivered a little as the cold air chilled the sweat on my body.

The woman sitting behind the front desk cast a suspicious look at Grace and me as we approached. We probably didn't look much like the people she was used to seeing come into the building. We were both dressed casually—me in khaki shorts and a simple burgundy Polo shirt, Grace in a pale-yellow summer maxi dress, the color contrasting nicely with her perpetual tan.

"I'm really missing Maka's badge right now," I muttered to Grace. She shushed me and walked toward the desk with a purposeful stride. She had this ability to take ownership of any space just with her walk that I'd always admired. It was as if her confidence coalesced entirely into her walk, and each step she took sent it out into the space around her, claiming the very ground itself.

I wished I had an ounce of the confidence Grace was able to project at a moment's notice. If I tried that, I'd just make a fool of myself.

"Can I help you?" The woman's voice was saccharine sweet, the sort of voice you only heard on phones or from people behind desks. The friendliness her tone suggested didn't reach her eyes; they were cautious, suspicious. Delgado had certainly groomed loyalty into his employees.

I thought about his assistant, Asher, who'd attempted to kill me, no doubt on Delgado's orders. Maybe loyalty wasn't the right word; more like fanaticism. Who would be so willing to kill for their boss?

And was Asher the only employee that was willing to do so? That wasn't a question I wanted to stake my life on. I just had to make sure not to turn my back on anyone in that snake pit.

"We're here to see Mr. Delgado. Sergio Delgado—though we'll take both of them if they're both available."

"They are both extremely busy, as I'm sure you can guess," the woman said carefully, a cool note slipping into her voice and undermining the friendly professionalism. "Do either of you have an appointment?"

"No," Grace answered in her own most professional voice. "They're going to want to meet with us, though, that I can promise you."

The woman raised her eyebrows in polite disbelief. "Why is that?"

"Because we're here about his fiancé's disappearance," I said, enjoying the way her professional veneer cracked, her eyes widening in surprise.

It did the trick and she picked up the phone and hit a few buttons. "Hey, Morgan. Is Mr. Delgado available now? I've got..." She stopped, looking our way and covering the phone with her hand. "I didn't catch your names."

"Gabe Maxfield and Grace Park."

If she'd heard those names before, she didn't give any indication, just returned to her phone. "I've got Gabe Maxfield and Grace Park here to speak with him. They say it's about Christine." She nodded, listening to the person on the other end of the phone. "All right."

She hung up, turning to us. "Mr. Delgado's assistant will check with him and see if he has time to see you. She'll call back."

"Thank you," I said, taking Grace's arm and leading her a little bit away from the desk. "You ready?"

"As I'll ever be," she answered.

"He's going to try to intimidate you. Don't let him get in your head."

Grace waved her hand dismissively. "Oh, I've never met with Manuel Delgado, but I've dealt with men like him before. Every woman has. Guys like him think they run the world, and that they are going to get everything they want simply because of who they are. In Manuel's case, it's because he has money. For some guys it's just the fact that they have a penis."

The front desk's phone rang, and Grace and I returned to it as the woman answered it. "Uh huh. All right. Thanks. You can go up," she said to us as she hung the phone up. "It's—"

"I remember. I've been there before," I said, making for the elevator.

A sense of panic built slowly in my stomach as the elevator rose, akin to the feeling that came as a roller coaster slowly ascended its track, where you knew that eventually it was going to plummet down again and all you could do was steel yourself in preparation.

I expected his new personal assistant to meet us when the elevators opened on the executive floor, but it was Manuel Delgado himself. He looked handsome standing there, framed in the elevator doorway, sharp features, his muscular form fitted perfectly in the suit. Again, I couldn't help but think about how he did everything for effect.

"Mr. Maxfield," Manuel Delgado said, his rich voice carrying. "What a pleasure to see you again. It's been far too long since I've been accused of murder." His eyes flashed toward Grace. "And this must be Ms. Park. A pleasure to meet you in person."

"I'm sure," Grace said dryly.

"Well, if you'll follow me, we can see to whatever it is you're here for."

He led us down the hall and to his office. It was as opulent as I remembered. "My assistant Morgan said you wanted to see me about my son's fiancé?"

"That's right, Mr. Delgado," I said. "We were hoping to talk to your son, as well."

"That won't be possible," Mr. Delgado said firmly. "He's busy. Any concerns you have can be directed to me."

"With all due respect, there's some questions we doubt you are capable of answering," Grace said, taking a seat across from Delgado's desk without an invitation. "Unless you know a lot more about your son's personal relationships than most fathers."

If Delgado was annoyed, he didn't show it. "Nevertheless, you'll have to settle for just me. Now, what's this all about?"

"We've been hired by Christine Hu's mother—" I started.

"Ah, yes, how is Helena doing?"

"Not so well, considering the circumstances," Grace sniped.

"We've been hired by Christine Hu's mother to look into the disappearance of her daughter. We wanted to talk to Sergio about that."

"I'm afraid you're not going to like this, but there's not any information to get. Sergio and I are as mystified by her behavior as Helena." Delgado spread his hands and leaned back in his chair as if that was the end of it.

"Mr. Delgado, I'm sure—"

I was cut off for the second time in as many minutes as Delgado's office door opened and Sergio Delgado came in. He looked exactly like his picture, though his suit was not quite as nice as the one he'd been wearing at his engagement announcement.

Delgado stood up at his entrance. "Sergio, *¿qué estás haciendo aquí?*"

"Morgan *me dijo que algunas personas estaban haciendo preguntas sobre* Christine," Sergio replied to whatever question his father asked him.

Manny Delgado did not look pleased at his son's presence. "*Vuelve a tu oficina. Yo me ocupo de esto.*"

I looked to Grace to see if she was following any of this. Her eyes were narrowed in concentration as she regarded the two men. I recalled that she'd taken Spanish all four years of college and wondered if she understood them.

"Christine is my fiancé," Sergio said, switching back to English, thankfully. "I should be here."

I made note of his use of "is" over "was." It didn't mean anything in and of itself, but there was a chance that if he knew something bad had befallen her, he might accidentally speak of her in the past tense.

Manny Delgado sighed and sat back down. Sergio must have taken it for acquiescence, because he turned to Grace and me. "I'm Sergio Delgado. Christine Hu is my fiancé." He shook first my hand and then Grace's.

"I'm Gabe, this is Grace. We work for a firm called Paradise Investigations. We were hired by Christine's mother, Helena Hu, to look into her disappearance."

Sergio went to stand behind the desk next to his father. "I'll try to help you as much as I can, but I doubt I'll be very helpful. I'd guess Mrs. Hu knows about as much as I do."

I highly doubt that, I thought wryly, but I kept the thought to myself. "Well, let's just start with the basics: do you know where Christine is?"

"Right to the point, I see. Okay. No, I don't know where Christine is. With money like hers, she could be pretty much anywhere in the world. If she wants to get lost, she has the resources to do so."

"When was the last time you saw her?" Grace asked after she started the recording app on her iPhone.

"Five nights ago," Sergio answered without hesitation. I couldn't help but be a little suspicious of the speed with which the answer came. He didn't even pause to think about it for a single second, like he'd been anticipating the question and had the answer already prepared. "We had dinner together and sat down to talk about some of the wedding plans. We were having trouble settling on a date for it."

"Was that the last time you spoke?" I asked.

"No. We talked on the phone the next night, and then again during the afternoon three days ago—the same day she disappeared. She was angry with me." Sergio lowered his eyes a little. "I was busy at the time, on my way to an important lunch meeting, and I kept brushing her aside. I felt bad about it, but thought that I would have a chance to apologize to her later that night. When I finished work, I tried to call her, but she didn't answer. Then I went to her apartment and saw that her bags were gone."

"What do you think happened to her, Mr. Delgado?" Grace prompted.

Sergio scowled. "I think she ran off with that sonofabitch personal assistant of hers, Travis."

"You didn't like Travis?" I surmised from his tone.

"I hated him the moment Christine hired him," Sergio confessed. "I saw the way he looked at her. I have no problem admitting that I can be a very jealous man. It's something I've tried to work on, for Christine's sake, but Travis Brent wanted my fiancé."

The anger in his voice sounded real enough, so I didn't doubt he genuinely felt Travis was a threat to his relationship. That didn't mean the story about Christine running off with him was true, of course. There were plenty of nonrequited crushes and feelings out there in the world.

"What did you do when you realized she was gone?"

"I called that bastard Travis. When he didn't answer, I reached out to the company that he contracted through. They told me Travis had taken a leave of absence that morning and told them he'd be out of the country." Sergio clenched his fists. "That's when I knew they'd run off together."

"My son left out something rather important," Manuel Delgado interrupted, reasserting his dominance in the conversation. "Maybe he's embarrassed by it, though I can't see why he would be. The issue that Christine was trying to discuss with him the day she disappeared was a prenuptial agreement. She didn't like it—as if it offended her honor. She wanted Sergio to withdraw it."

"Sergio, was the prenup a point of contention in your relationship?" Grace asked.

Manuel Delgado bristled. "Digging for motivation, Ms. Park? I'm afraid my son has answered all of the relevant questions—which he didn't have to do—and this meeting is over."

"We're just trying to get some answers, Mr. Delgado," I said, rising.

"I know what your search for answers entails, Mr. Maxfield," Manuel sneered. "I'm familiar with it, as I'm sure you recall. Last time your quest for answers included accusing me of arranging murder, now you're going to do the same to my son? I think not. You should leave."

"Of course," Grace said primly, striding toward the door. "Thank you so much for your time, both of you."

"Mr. Maxfield, Ms. Park," Manuel Delgado called before we opened the door. "Any future questions you have can be referred to our family attorney. I believe you've met."

I couldn't hold back a smirk. "So we have." The last time I'd encountered their attorney, I'd bested him. He'd have to do better than that if he wanted to intimidate me.

The look on my face must not have set well with Delgado, because his lips dipped into a frown. "Let me offer a friendly warning to the two of you: I know I have a reputation as a ruthless businessman, and it's well-earned. However, that's *nothing* compared to how I am when people I love are threatened."

I met his gaze steadily. "Don't worry, Mr. Delgado, you'll find that I'm exactly the same way."

THAT NIGHT I sat curled up on Maka's sofa next to him. It was movie night, and we were watching some comedy about spies with Melissa McCarthy. My mind was elsewhere, though, and I hadn't even really paid any attention to the movie. I couldn't recall the faintest thing about the plot.

I wish I could say it was this new case that was on my mind, but it wasn't. I was thinking about the phone call from my mother. I often described her—if I ever did—as the most nonmaternal person to ever give birth. She was emotionally cold, distant. The only actual emotion I could actually remember her exhibiting was disdain. Yet, on the phone she sounded...almost upset, like my refusing to see them was more than just some flaw in their plan.

"Okay," Maka said suddenly, gently nudging my shoulder. "That was legitimately one of the funniest things I've seen in a comedy movie in years, and not even a reaction from you. *You* picked this movie, remember?"

"I'm sorry, my mind's just wandering off today."

"You were fine when you brought me lunch. What's going on? Your meeting with Delgado shake you up that much?"

I made a noise in the back of my throat. "No way I'd give Delgado the satisfaction of getting to me. That's not what this is about."

Maka shifted positions so we could look at each other, much better for conversing. His eyes kept glancing toward the television every now and then, though, so I reached over and hit the button on the game controller that paused the movie for him.

He rewarded me with a quick smile of thanks before pressing on. "Okay, then, what's it about?"

Part of me didn't want to have this conversation. If I told him, that meant I had to talk about it and anything involving my parents was an unpleasant enough conversation. The last thing I wanted to do was waste my precious time with Maka talking about *them*. I considered making something up, but Maka was a damn good detective, and he'd know it for a lie the moment I said it.

I had no choice but to be honest. "I got a phone call right after lunch. It was my mother."

Maka sucked his teeth in sympathy at that. We'd had discussions about my parents before, and he knew how much of a rough subject it would be. "How did that go?"

"About as well as you'd expect," I said, playing it off lightly. "It didn't last very long."

I could see Maka wrestling with something before he finally spoke. "What did she want?"

"To tell me they're in Hawai'i," I answered as nonchalantly as I could manage. It was a defense mechanism I'd learned dealing with having the people I had for parents. If you pretended that something didn't bother you long enough, you started to believe it yourself. "Here in Honolulu, in fact."

I summarized the short conversation quickly, keeping my eyes mostly on the frozen image of the paused movie, where Melissa McCarthy was on the run from some guys with guns.

"So that's that?" Maka asked when I finished.

"Of course it is. Why wouldn't it be?"

There was another moment of inner debate that I could see behind Maka's eyes, and I knew I wasn't going to like whatever he brought up.

"I know your history with them, but would it be the worst thing in the world to at least hear what it is they have to say?"

"Yes," I said flatly. "It might actually be the worst thing in the world. I took so much crap from them as a child. I was never what they wanted in their eyes, only good for keeping my grandfather invested in them. Then, when he died, they saw me as a potential well of money. They've never found value in me as their son. I don't know why I should give them the benefit of the doubt."

"People change a lot in ten years," Maka said gently.

"They didn't change at all in the seventeen years that I lived with them," I said stubbornly, "so why should I believe they changed in ten?"

Some people didn't change. This was one issue that maybe Maka just couldn't understand, with his seemingly perfect family. Sure, I knew they had their issues, because there wasn't a family out there who didn't, but still I felt that the relative normality of his family left him ill-equipped to deal with the complexities of a family with the level of disfunction mine had.

"Is this about getting back at them for the way they treated you?"

"What? No! This isn't about revenge. This is about me refusing to engage with their nonsense. Now come on." I pointed at the television. "Let's finish the movie."

"Do you even know what's going on in the movie?" Maka challenged.

"Sure, I do. Melissa McCarthy is a spy, and now there's bad guys after her."

"What about Jude Law?"

I blinked. "Jude Law is in this movie?"

"How did you not notice Jude Law?"

I shrugged in the face of his accusatory tone. "I'm not as into the *haole* as you are, that's how, I guess. I'm going to unpause the movie now."

"Fine, but when the movie's over, we're going to talk about why this thing with your parents is actually bothering you."

"Fine. Or," I added slyly, "I can think of a few other things for us to do that are way better than talking about my parental issues."

"Gabe Maxfield, are you bribing me with sex?"

"I'm trying to, but you're not making it easy."

Maka pretended to think about the offer for a moment. "Fine. But we're going to talk about this eventually."

"Not as long as I can keep up with your sex drive, we won't."

AT JUST AFTER five in the morning, I was jarred from a dream I remembered enjoying though the details of it faded rapidly from my memory, like smoke clearing in the wake of a breeze.

It took me a moment to realize that the cause of my waking was the persistent vibration of my phone on Maka's bedside table.

"Someone better be dead," Maka grumbled from his part of the bed, his head buried under his pillow.

I shared his sentiments. The number on the phone was one I didn't recognize, but it was a Hawai'i area code. For a moment, I wondered if my mother was again attempting to contact me from the hotel phone? It seemed unlikely, even for them. My disdain for mornings had existed for all of my life. Mother knew an early morning phone call was *not* the way to get on my good side.

"Are you going to answer that or are you using it as a vibrator?" Maka growled at me from beneath his pillow. I realized I was just staring at my phone.

"Sorry." My voice sounded strange to my ears, still laden down with the weight of sleep. I answered the phone and held it to my ear. "What?" Considering I didn't know who it was I might should have been nicer, but considering the hour whoever it was would have to get over it.

"Is this Gabe Maxfield of Paradise Investigations?" It was a man's voice, one that sounded far too awake for my tastes.

"You're calling my number, not even sure I'm who you're trying to reach?" I made no effort to keep the annoyance out of my voice. "That seems not smart." *And dangerous*, I added silently. Certainly if I could kill by sheer force of will alone this guy would already be dead.

"Well, is it?"

Later I would blame my brain for misfiring in that moment and missing the perfect opportunity to say no and send whoever this was on their figurative way.

Instead, like an idiot, I said, "It is. Now what the hell do you want?"

"I want to ask you why you're investigating the split-up of Christine Hu and Sergio Delgado."

I should have expected that, given the veiled hint Manuel Delgado had thrown our way.

"Not going to say that I am, but who the hell are you—" Maka grunted beside me, and I lowered my voice. "—and why is it any of your business *what* I investigate?"

"Let me start over. My name is Braeden Jeffords. I'm a reporter."

Great, a reporter. He'd just said the one thing that could make me dislike him as much as if he'd been one of Delgado's goons. Reporters were bad for business. They ended up drawing a spotlight, turning even a cut and dry case into a high-profile fiasco. Sure, stories about us gave us a boost to our business, but it did come at a cost.

"I'm not about to talk to a reporter about a case like this. Do you think I'm stupid? Who do you write for, anyway?"

"I'm more of a...a reporter in images," Braeden Jeffords replied, dancing around my question.

I was in no mood for games, and the longer I was awake at that ungodly hour, the further south that mood went. "Which would make you a photographer."

"I'm a photographer who tells stories with pictures." Now Braeden sounded defensive. "I focus on stories about celebrities."

I was disliking this guy more and more. "So you're a paparazzi."

"Actually the singular form is paparazzo," Braeden corrected me. God, this guy just didn't know how to read the air at all. "If you are—"

"Listen, Mr. Jeffords, I can't think of a single reason I'd ever talk to you about *anything*. If you're looking for any scandalous details, you can just forget it. If I were actually working the case, why would I jeopardize a paying job just to talk to some celebrity leech?"

"Just listen! If you *are* looking into the Delgado case, I've got something important to—"

I hung the phone up before he could finish that sentence, tossing the phone back onto the nightstand. What I wanted to do was toss it out the window, but I knew that awake me would regret that, so I didn't.

I hoped I remembered to applaud myself for my restraint in the morning.

"Who was that?" Maka asked, rolling onto his back.

"Paparazzi," I mumbled, settling back down to go back to sleep.

"You know what?" Maka's voice grew fainter with every word as he drifted back into sleep. "You've really got to think about changing your number."

Chapter Four

NEEDLESS TO SAY, the next day found me in a pretty bad mood. I was testy in the mornings under the best of circumstances, with a full night's sleep. Today it had seemed like I'd barely gotten my eyes closed again when the alarm went off for both Maka and me to get up.

For his part, Maka seemed perfectly fine. Then again, he was, unfortunately, a morning person, something that had taken some time for the two of us to reconcile, though we were still working out the kinks of that.

Maka, having come to recognize my moods, gave me my morning space, speaking to me only to say good morning and goodbye. It was the little things in a relationship that you came to respect the most, I'd discovered.

I left the house not long after Maka and spent most of the drive contemplating telling Mrs. Neidermeyer not to come into work. I might blow a gasket if I had to hear the two of them bickering.

I arrived at work and let out a low curse. For the second time in two days there was a strange car parked in front of Paradise Investigations. What the hell was going on? Didn't anyone think to make an appointment anymore?

I drove by the car slowly, hoping to catch a glimpse inside, but it was parked in the first spot, a difficult angle for me coming into the small parking lot. I did notice a barcode on the rear window, though, like it was on the shelf at some store. It was a simple car, gray, the sort that you could see just about anywhere on the road.

Oh shit.

A rental car.

I pulled into my usual parking space and rested my head on the steering wheel. What I wanted to do was bang my head against it and hope that the resulting concussion would prevent me from having to deal with this.

In the rearview mirror I saw the rental car's door open and my mother step out from behind the wheel. She was easily recognizable: she had the exact same hairdo she'd sported in 2008. I actually couldn't remember a time she *didn't* have her hair in what looked like a style that would have been perfect on one of those daytime soap operas, though there were pictures that proved she'd done something different with it at one point.

Another thing that hadn't changed, along with the hair, was the fact that the woman had no idea how to take a hint. It would not have crossed her mind that coming to see me was a bad idea, because she had something she wanted and that was all that mattered. Of course I would bend to her will eventually; the whole world seemed to do that for most of her life—or at least since she married my father.

The benefits of a husband with name value.

Well, I can't hide in my car forever. As disheartening a prospect as it was, I needed to get out and actually go into work. Hopefully I could avoid the full brunt of Hurricane Vivian by hurrying inside. She'd have to understand I was busy. And if she didn't, oh well.

I took a deep breath to ready myself, like someone about to jump into ice-cold water—considering my mother's icy personality it wasn't that far-off of a simile—and got out of the car, eyes on the prize that was the office door.

Mrs. Neidermeyer wasn't in yet, which meant I would have to unlock the door to get in, which would increase the amount of time I needed to spend in my mother's presence, but it couldn't be helped.

"Gabriel." Mother started toward me, but I sidestepped her, still making for the door.

"I'm not going to bother asking how you found my work."

"Listen, I don't like the idea of having to ambush you at your job," she said defensively, falling into step beside me. "But after the way you acted on the phone yesterday, what choice did I have?"

I fished my keys out of my pocket as I neared the step up to the door. "Oh, I don't know, Mother, how about respecting my wishes to *not* have to deal with you? That was an option, though I'm betting it didn't even cross your mind."

"Gabe, don't be this way."

"What way is that?" I jammed the key into the door.

"You know exactly what I mean!" she snapped, and I thought, *There she is, there's the Vivian Maxfield I know.* "You've always been this way—sullen and selfish."

I stopped midturn of the doorknob and rounded on her. I knew I shouldn't, knew that engaging with her would get me nowhere, but it was a defense mechanism I hadn't yet learned to override.

"I'm selfish? Me, that's what you're saying? Like it was selfish of me to not surrender control of my inheritance from Grandpa to you?"

"We wanted to look out for you!"

"No, you wanted to look out for *you*. How much of that money—*my* money—would I have left if I'd signed control over to you, huh? And just what would I have had to do to get even a share of it? You guys wanted the money to fill your own pockets and to hold over me and ensure that you could keep control over me, make me live the way you wanted me to."

"Your grandfather gave you that money to spite your father! He used you against us and you just let him!" Mother took an unsteady breath, her plastic surgery-smooth cheeks red. "I didn't come here to argue with you, Gabriel."

"Then why did you come here?"

"I came here to reconnect. I know there are a lot of things I haven't done right in my life, and—"

"Are you dying?" I asked bluntly. "Is that what this is about? Some death-bed effort to atone for being a shitty parent?" It was the only thing I could think of that would make sense, the only thing that could possibly explain her presence.

"What? No, it's nothing like that. I'm not sick, neither is your father."

"Oh, well then." I pushed the door open and stepped inside, quickly starting to shut it behind me so she couldn't follow me in.

"Gabe, we just want to talk to you," she pleaded very uncharacteristically.

"Well, I don't really have anything to say back, and I can't imagine you have anything to say that I will actually want to hear. I'm sorry the two of you came all this way for nothing."

I closed the door before she could respond, turning the lock to make sure she didn't attempt to follow me inside, which I would not have put past her.

She knocked on the door a few times, called my name, but I ignored her. She must have given up, because she finally called. "We're staying at the Aqua Palms Waikiki," and then I heard the sound of her heels on the concrete as she walked away.

I exhaled a breath I didn't realize I was holding and made my way back to the safety and silence of my office. Well, silence for as long as I had it. It wouldn't be long before Grace and Mrs. Neidermeyer were there to draw me back into the world of my commitments and work.

"Gabe, you here?" Grace's voice called out to me from the front of the office.

I saved a snarky remark—I mean, my car was out there, wasn't it?—and just called back. "Yes. In my office."

I heard Grace's footsteps as she came back. I was surprised to find that she had on high heels. She didn't usually wear that sort of footwear to work. Maybe she was hoping Jin would stop by.

"Why was the door locked?"

"We had an unexpected visitor when I got here," I answered, not really wanting to go into it.

Not going into it, though, resulted in Grace freaking out a little, which wasn't surprising, given our history. "Are you okay?"

"Not that kind of visitor, calm down. It was my mother. Apparently being rejected over the phone wasn't enough to make her get the message, she needed it to be done in person, too."

Grace looked like she wanted to say something for a moment but decided against it. I wondered what it would have been, but we were distracted by the sound of the phone ringing in the front.

"Is Mrs. Neidermeyer here?" I asked.

"She wasn't when I came in," Grace replied. We both found that to be unusual; Mrs. Neidermeyer might not dress professionally, and she might forget to tell us that she booked clients, or forget important information like who our appointments were actually with, but she was *always* on time.

Grace went out to answer the phone while I dialed Mrs. Neidermeyer's number on my cell. It rang four times before she answered.

"Hello?"

"Mrs. Neidermeyer, it's Gabe. We were concerned since you hadn't made it to work yet."

"Oh, I'm sorry, Gabe. I forgot to call. I'll be a little late. I'm at the doctor's office right now getting my ankle x-rayed."

The idea of a woman Mrs. Neidermeyer's age having a broken bone was unsettling. She was at that point where recovery became much less likely.

"Are you all right?"

"I'm fine, I'm fine. Pretty sure I just sprained my ankle at my pole dancing class last night. Can never be too sure, you know? I'll be in to work as soon as I'm done here."

"Don't overdo it," I cautioned, trying my best *not* to imagine Gertrude Neidermeyer dancing on a stripper pole. "Maybe you should take a day of rest."

"What, and watch *The Young and the Restless* put Victor in jail for the two hundredth time right after he remarries the same woman he's married and divorced every six months or so for the last forty years?" She let out a noise that told me exactly what she thought of that. "No, thank you. I'll be in to work. Besides, I'm DVRing the episode."

"Okay, see you later then," I said, hanging up just as Grace came back into my office. "Mrs. Neidermeyer's at the doctor. She twisted her ankle."

"Doing something completely inappropriate for a woman her age, no doubt."

I nodded. "Pole dancing."

Grace made a face. "Gross. I didn't want to know that."

"I sure as hell wasn't going to be the only one with the image of her pole dancing burned into their brain," I said dryly. "Who was on your end?"

"That was Mrs. Hu. She's on her way over with a few more things for us."

"Maybe Mrs. Neidermeyer will stay out long enough for her to come by and leave."

Grace chuckled. "That would be nice."

It took Helena Hu half an hour to arrive, and I put that time to good use working on paperwork and expense reports, filing everything away properly for tax season soon. A case like this was likely to consume a lot of our time, and I didn't want the paperwork to get neglected or build up, because that would just mean a long night at the end of the case.

Grace and I usually took several cases, ones we could each work while occasionally consulting each other if we needed help. A case like this, though, would require both of our constant attention. It put all of our other tasks on hold. It was a good thing we weren't hurting for money, since we'd received the reward for returning the stolen Japanese art. We'd been thrifty with it, planning our purchases carefully and saving as much money as we could.

I was just finishing up an expense report for a job we'd completed two weeks before when Grace called to me that Helena was there. This time it wasn't in a limousine but an extremely shiny Lexus, something only somewhat less noticeable than the limo. I also noticed she was alone and wondered why.

I thought about the paparazzo who called me that morning. He probably knew about our involvement in this case because of the flashy way she'd arrived the previous day. Is that what Helena had intended? Did she want it to be known that she'd sought us out? If so, why?

Maybe it was a message for the Delgados. Whatever her reasons, it was clear to me that she had an agenda. Then again, I guess everyone did. I just didn't like the idea of getting caught up in the agenda of people with money.

"I apologize for being late," she said when she stepped through the door. She was dressed in muted colors, though the clothes were still designer.

"No worries," Grace said kindly. "Why don't we go back to my office and we can talk about what it is you've got for us, Mrs. Hu."

"Please call me Helena. I really hate the formalities. They make me feel so stodgy and old."

We made our way to Grace's office this time, Grace and I reversing the positions we were in the previous day. "What did you want to speak to us about?" I asked once she was settled.

"Last night I was thinking and I realized it might be useful to give you this." She pulled a folded-up piece of paper from her purse. "This is a list of Christine's close friends, those who would know the most about her and could best answer questions for you."

"Thank you." I took the proffered piece of paper and placed it on the desk next to me.

"Then there's this." She held up a key. "It's my spare key to Christine's apartment. I thought maybe there would be something there that might be helpful. I haven't..." her voice faltered for a moment. "I haven't been able to bring myself to go there yet, not since I knew she disappeared. It's apartment seven-nineteen."

She hesitated for a moment before she handed the key over, as if the very act itself was painful. It probably was. Once it left her hand, she shuddered visibly and then took a deep breath.

"If you need anything else, you know where to reach me. You have my number."

"Actually, there was something we needed to ask you about," Grace said before she could stand up and leave. "Doing our groundwork yesterday we went and spoke with the Delgados."

Helena's smile was stretched and weary. "Let me guess, they mentioned the prenuptial agreement?"

She's a damn clever woman, I thought admiringly. I had no doubt that she'd expected us to do just that and expected Delgado to respond precisely how he had. I wondered how many steps ahead of everyone else she was. It was like playing chess with someone who'd already claimed victory in a certain number of moves. Delgado didn't have any idea who he was dealing with, I suspected.

"He did. Said that Christine was angry about it, wanted to convince Sergio to abandon it."

Helena shook her head. "Christine had no problem with the prenup. We had our family lawyers look it over and found it to be very basic—and provide protections both ways, which was important to us."

"What do you mean provided protection both ways?" I asked.

"While I'm sure it's a fact that Manuel Delgado played down, Christine is worth more money than Sergio Delgado is. The prenuptial agreement would prevent Sergio from claiming any of her assets, as well. It was mutually beneficial, so there was no reason Christine would have protested it. Any indication otherwise is misleading."

Grace drummed her fingers on her desk thoughtfully. "Why, then, would Delgado make such a claim?"

"You're the private detectives. You tell me."

It wasn't that hard to guess, though if course I couldn't be sure. "Part of it is about image, I'm sure—when people hear that a woman was asked to sign a prenup it automatically makes them put the man in the superior position in their minds. It empowers him and weakens her."

Helena nodded, looking pleased. "Yes. I think there's more to it than that, though. It provides convenient so-called motive for Christine to run away, does it not? It paints her as a gold digger who, when she couldn't get her way, gave up and ran off."

"That's not a hard narrative to disprove, though," I pointed out. "All someone has to do is put in the most basic effort to examine their finances and see it's not true."

"Yes, but who's going to put in the effort to do that? Society as a whole in this country, particularly because it's dominated by white straight men, is all too willing to accept that narrative with no challenge. No one will bother because *obviously* it's true, because they've seen movies and television shows where that happens. They've convinced themselves this sort of thing happens all the time. It's just a more subtle form of engrained misogyny."

There was nothing more to say to that, because she was right, and I could see that.

With nothing else to discuss, Helena excused herself, leaving Grace and me there to stare at and contemplate the key to Christine's apartment. Neither one of us needed to ask about our next step, since it was clear what it should be.

"Should we wait for Mrs. Neidermeyer?" Grace asked uncharacteristically. "In case someone tries to call in, I mean."

I waved her concern away. "Just take the phone off the hook. They'll think we're busy and keep trying to call back. Unless you really want to see what Mrs. Neidermeyer is wearing today."

Grace stood up quickly, snatching Christine's apartment key off the table. "Let's go."

CHRISTINE HU'S APARTMENT was near Koko Crater Botanical Gardens, and from the looks of it, cost triple what my condo did. Given that I could hear the sound of the ocean in the distance, I imagined that the upper levels could actually see the ocean from their windows.

The door had an automatic lock, but next to it was a box with numbers so you could call up to the room you were visiting as well as a key slot. I took a chance and inserted the key into the slot and turned it. There was a buzzing sound followed by a whirring noise and then the door clicked open.

Grace and I went inside. I was surprised by how spartan the main entrance was, but figured that the apartments themselves would be more lavish. It wasn't a hotel, after all; not many people spent that much time in the lobby of their apartment building.

We took the elevator to the seventh floor. As it made its way slowly up, Grace turned to me and asked, "Did your mother say what made them come to Hawai'i to see you?"

I was caught off guard by the sudden turn to my family. "Uh, no. I'm not that interested in *why*, to be honest. I'd really like to pretend that they aren't here. I did ask if one of them was dying, she said no."

"Oh, okay." Again there was that look on her face, like there was more that she wanted to say. What was she holding back?

I narrowed my eyes at her. "Why do you ask?"

"What? No reason. Just making conversation."

I didn't push her on the issue, even though she was acting strange. At that point, we needed to focus on the job and not my personal life.

The hallway was nicer, resembling a hotel in its look and feel. The floor was softly carpeted, the walls a soothing shade of tan, each door bearing a brass placard with its number. I half expected to see an ice machine tucked to the side somewhere.

We had to turn down two hallways before we finally came to Christine's apartment. I peeked down the third hallway and caught sight of the same elevator we'd come in on. Naturally.

Grace fumbled with the key in the door for a moment. As she swung the door open one of the neighbors emerged from their apartment, dressed in a business suit and looking like he was in a hurry.

He gave Grace and me a funny look as he passed us on his way to the elevator. I just smiled and nodded politely, hurrying Grace inside and closing the door behind me.

"Must feel weird, huh," Grace remarked.

"What must feel weird?"

"Using a key to get in instead of breaking in."

I pushed her on into the main room. "One time, I've broken into a place—not even breaking, really just entering—*one* time, and that was to get *you* off the hook for murder, remember? Maybe you'd like to be a little more grateful."

"That was months ago. My gratefulness has worn off."

Christine's apartment was spacious, as I'd expected. Directly across from the door was the dining area, and beyond that two panes of floor-to-ceiling windows. They didn't look out onto the ocean because of the side of the building we were on, but they had a nice view of the city itself and mountains in the distance.

To our left was the kitchen area and to the right the living room and a door that must lead to the bedroom. A bookshelf stood against the wall next to that door, brimming with books. From the doorway, I could see that quite a few of them were Stephen King titles, so Christine was likely a horror fan.

"It's so weird being in someone else's house," Grace remarked, heading into the kitchen area. "I feel bad for invading her privacy like this."

"We're doing it to find her," I reminded Grace, following her into the kitchen. "We can apologize to her when she's back at home."

An island stood in the middle of the kitchen area, a vase with fake flowers and a fruit bowl in the center of it. There was also a stack of mail and a memo pad on the corner closest to the refrigerator. The refrigerator sported several pictures, and I moved to look at those while Grace picked up the mail and other pieces of paper.

The photographs people keep displayed tell a story, and Christine's told the story of a happy young woman. Most were of Christine and two other women about her age, one Asian and one Caucasian—they were probably at the top of the list that Helena gave us—but there were also several photos of Christine and Helena together, photos of a much younger Christine with a man who must have been her father, and two pictures of Christine and Sergio together, one obviously taken on the day that Sergio proposed to her.

I had a flashback of the last time I'd examined someone's life from the pictures on their refrigerator. It had been in the dark of night, because I hadn't wanted anyone to see me, and I hadn't been invited into her home.

"Sergio and Christine look genuinely happy in all of these pictures," I commented to Grace over my shoulder. If there *was* something wrong between them, it didn't translate to photos."

I took one last look at Christine's smiling face and turned back to Grace. "What do you have?"

"Lots of stuff," she answered. She held up a stack of envelopes. "These are different invoices for the wedding—caterer, flowers, cake— and they're *all* expensive, and they've all already been paid. I didn't do the math, but just looking at some of them tells me this wedding is already in the tens of thousands and rising quickly. These don't include the venue or the wedding dress or decorations."

She put the invoices down and picked up a spiral notebook that had been under them. "This notebook is full of wedding planning and notes. Things like 'Ask Sergio about his cake preference' and 'wedding dress shopping 2/1.'"

She picked up the top invoice. "Look at this, it's for the bouquets. It was paid the day before Christine disappeared. Thirty-five hundred dollars."

I thought that through for a moment. "If she was going to run off with this Travis guy, why would she pay this?"

Grace pointed her finger at me. "My thoughts exactly."

While I had never believed that Christine had run off, this settled it in my mind. Paying wedding bills and diligently planning the wedding wasn't the action of someone who intended to run out on it.

"We should check the bedroom, see if there's anything in there."

In the bedroom we found basically nothing. Her closet was mostly cleaned out, as were her dressers. There was a desk in front of the one window in the bedroom, situated so Christine could sit at it and look out. There was a telltale space where a laptop likely sat, though it was nowhere to be seen.

Grace took in all of it, hands on her hips. "Someone worked really hard to make it look like Christine ran off."

"That would be child's play for Delgado, knowing what we know about him."

"How much are you willing to bet Sergio Delgado has a key to this place?"

"Never make bets you know you're going to lose," I said with a chuckle. "That's definitely one I don't want to make. Any sign of a cell phone?"

Grace looked everywhere a cell phone might be placed and shook her head. "I don't see a charger for it, either."

"They really did do a thorough job," I mused.

Someone knocked on the front door—three hard, firm knocks that made both Grace and me jump. Panic bubbled in me, hot and tight, settling in my chest and constricting my lungs. My first immediate thought was that we were in danger. If Delgado had us tailed, and thought we were getting close to exposing whatever happened, then he'd have no problem having us taken care of—he'd practically said as much when he warned us not to go after his family.

The knocking came again, harder this time, and Grace mouthed, *What do we do?*

Before I could answer her a deep, booming voice called out through the door. "This is the police. Open the door, please."

What were the police doing there? I made my way hesitantly to the front door, peering through the peephole to make sure it wasn't some trick to get us to open up. Sure enough, there was a uniformed police officer standing outside the door.

Sending a shrug Grace's way, I opened the door.

The officer gave no introductions, no friendly greetings. He just got right to why he was there. "Are either of you the owner of this apartment?"

"No, we're not. We were hired by *the owner* of this apartment."

"We received a report that the two of you broke in," the officer went on, like he didn't even hear me.

"No, like I said, we were hired by the owner."

Grace dug the apartment key from her pocket and held it up for the officer to see. "We have a key."

"Given to us by the *owner of the apartment*," I added, in case he was having a hard time processing this.

"And if I were to call—" He checked a small notepad. "—this Christine Hu, she would be able to verify this?"

"I doubt she'd be able to verify anything. She's missing, which is why we're here."

"You can call her mother, though," Grace chimed in, thumping me in the small of my back, probably to tell me to rein in my sarcasm. "She's the one who gave us the key. Helena Hu."

The police officer glowered at us. "Helena Hu isn't the name on the apartment lease. Her permission doesn't matter to me."

"We're private investigators," I said more patiently. "Christine Hu has gone missing, and we've been hired by her mother to look into it."

"That's something for the police," said the officer, sounding bored.

"The police are investigating, but Helena Hu wanted us to—"

"Listen, I don't want to waste anymore time with this. The two of you need to leave immediately, or I'm going to arrest you."

"For what?" Grace demanded indignantly.

The officer stiffened at Grace's tone. "I don't know, how about trespassing? Or interfering with an ongoing police investigation? You private investigators think you're so great. What you need to do is go on and leave the investigating to the real police officers. Stick to taking pictures of horny old men and their mistresses."

Grace opened her mouth to say something, and before she could I cleared my throat loudly and tried on my most placating voice. "Of course, Officer. Sorry to inconvenience you. Come on, Grace."

I took her by the hand and had to tug her out behind me, stopping only to lock the door under the watchful eye of the police officer. Door secured, we hurried toward the elevator. I didn't look back, but I could feel the officer's eyes on us until the elevator doors pinged open and closed again behind us.

Chapter Five

I WAS GRATEFUL to finally get home that evening. I felt drained from the early morning phone call and my run-in with my mother. The silence of my condo slipped around me like the comforting embrace of a friend.

Today being Friday meant Maka would be coming over tonight and bringing takeout, and I looked forward to it. I hoped he picked up loco moco from one of the many food trucks I'd come to love.

Checking the time and seeing I had about two hours before Maka finished work, I decided to just veg out and do nothing in front of the television. I stopped halfway to sitting down and thought about the mail. I hadn't checked it when I came in like I usually did.

I went back to the door to collect it before I got comfortable on the couch. The mailbox to my condo was beside the door, a rectangular box mounted on the wall.

As I craned my neck to peer inside the mailbox, the hairs on the back of my neck stood on end. I looked around, trying to find out where the strange sensation I had was coming from. At first, I didn't see anything out of the ordinary and assumed my encounter with Delgado earlier had left me shaken.

Then I saw them, my hand halfway into the mailbox. Two men were standing casually next to a car in the parking lot, engaged in a conversation. Both were bulky white men, both with dark hair, one longer, one kept shorter and slicked back out of his face with gel, the other longer and tied tightly with a ponytail. They wore dark sunglasses.

I never saw them look my way, but I couldn't shake the feeling that they were watching me. I'd never seen either of them before, which was odd, because I was sure I'd met or at least seen everyone who lived in the condominium complex.

Are they spies sent by Delgado to follow me? I hadn't noticed them before, but that didn't mean they hadn't been there. For all I knew, they'd been with me ever since Helena came to give us the job the previous day.

I hurried back inside, making sure to deadbolt the door behind me. Never could be too careful. But if Delgado thought he could frighten me away from this job, he was highly mistaken. If anything, his bullying attempts made me more determined to dig into this case and find the truth. If Delgado didn't want me looking into it, then there was bound to be something there. Delgado had wriggled his slimy way free of blame for Carrie's murder, but this would be harder for him, I hoped.

We just needed to find one piece of evidence to nail him. The presence of the men outside my condo made me think that evidence existed, too.

I sat down on the couch, turning the television on, though I didn't pay much attention to what was on the screen. My mind remained outside with those two guys who were no doubt stalking me.

I resisted the urge to get up and go to the window and look out at them. I wasn't going to become that person who sat behind the blinds. I would not allow paranoia to set in in my own home. It had taken a lot of time to reclaim the comfortable feeling of safety in the place after I was attacked just weeks after my arrival in Hawai'i. I wasn't giving that sense of security up again for anything or anyone.

But they were still out there. I didn't need to look through the blinds to know that. Maybe they were no longer standing there pretending to be engaged in a casual conversation, but they were there somewhere. In their car, watching my door, perhaps.

I had to assume they were just eyes—Delgado's way of keeping track of where Grace and I were in the investigation. If they had been anything else, they would have made a move already. That fact didn't really make me feel better, but it was something.

What should have been a relaxing two hours in front of the television turned out to be anything but, and by the end of it, I was even more tightly wound than I had been to begin with. It was a struggle to not freak out at every little noise I heard. Once I noticed the footsteps of one of my neighbors and convinced myself it was the two men, tired of waiting.

I managed not to freak out at the sound of Maka sliding his key into the lock, but only just. I used his arrival as an excuse to look out at the parking lot, rising to meet him at the door, a smile plastered on my lips.

"Woah, this is unexpected," Maka said, taking my greeting in with wide eyes. "What, I get door greeting treatment now? Where's my cocktail?"

"What?" I asked, focusing just around his shoulder. It was evening now, and the shadow of the condo stretched long into the parking lot, but I couldn't miss the bright red flare of a cigarette as someone inside a car I was unfamiliar with took a drag from it.

That was them, no doubt about it.

Maka closed the door behind him. "I figured if you were going to go all *Mad Men* and greet me at the door after work, you'd be carrying a drink for me. Especially since I brought you *this*." He victoriously brandished the brown sack. The smell of its contents struck me and my stomach asserted itself over my brain, hunger driving the unease off.

"Loco moco from the Taco Moco truck?" I asked hopefully.

"Of course. It's your favorite."

Maka went through his usual post-work ritual—removed his sidearm and placed it on the peg in the wall near the door he'd put in specifically for that purpose. His badge and car keys went on the small table near the door. He made his way to my small square of a dining room table and laid the bag down. I skipped to it, rolling the top open, already salivating in anticipation while Maka grabbed silverware.

"You know," I said, taking out the two large Styrofoam boxes that contained our dinner, "whoever thought about combining Mexican and Hawaiian food was brilliant."

"Yeah, but what does it become, you know? It's not Hawaiian, it's not Mexican. It's something else." Maka took his customary seat at the table facing the door. It was a cop thing, he'd said when I first noticed he always did it. Something about never putting your back to an exit.

I sat down at the seat next to him, the door to my left. Usually I sat directly across from him, back to the door, but I was starting to think there might be something to this whole not turning your back thing. Maka quirked an eyebrow at my choice but didn't say anything. It probably helped that his mouth was already full of egg, hamburger, rice, and gravy.

"Maybe we should call it something new, then," I said, opening my box and grabbing the fork he'd brought. "Like Mexiwaiian?" Maka made a face at that. "Okay, how about Hawexican?"

"That's better than Mexiwaiian, but it's still bad," Maka said after swallowing. "Shit, I forgot drinks."

"I'll get them," I said, knowing he was tired from work. I grabbed two bottles of Heineken from the refrigerator and popped the tops off with a bottle opener.

"So, how was your day after that rousing start?" Maka asked after downing about half of his beer in one long pull. I made a noise of disgust deep in my throat. "That bad, huh?"

I told him about my run-in with my mother, and then our encounter with the police. I started to tell him about the two men outside when I came home but decided not to. He was protective enough as it was, and worried enough, and I didn't want to make it any worse.

Besides, all I had to go on was my instincts, and god knew how bad those could be. I hadn't seen Trevor coming at all, had I?

"What about you?" I asked to turn the attention away from me. I knew he wouldn't give me a lot of details, because he couldn't, but he could throw some general things my way.

"Finally wrapped up the Orenfield murder," he said carefully. "Made an arrest. Bout time, too; it's been three months."

"Who did it?" I asked, smiling innocently when he shot me that look that said *You know I'm not going to tell you.* "Fine, I'll just read about it in the paper like everyone else."

"You don't read the paper," Maka pointed out, bemused.

"That's because *no one* reads newspapers anymore! And fine, I'll hear it on the news then, like everyone else. What's the point of a cop boyfriend if I can't know all the fun details early?"

"You and I have very different definitions of 'fun details,' babe," Maka said. He finished off his dinner while I was only at the halfway mark, but it didn't surprise me. He was an incredibly fast eater, wolfing his food down in bites that should have choked him. Seeing my progress, he said, "Mind if I take a shower real quick while you're still eating?"

"Sure, go ahead. Don't forget to put a towel down this time," I added as he went back into the bathroom.

"I forgot *one time*," he called back. "When are you going to let that go?"

"When you remember to put the towel down."

He muttered something in response that I couldn't hear. We both had very different methods with the way we chose to live, and having both been living alone for as long as we had, we were set in our ways. We weren't entirely incompatible, but we would require compromise if we progressed further in the relationship.

Thankfully, neither of us was ready for the "let's live together" step. I liked him a lot, and I was really happy, but that was a big step, one I took too quickly with Trevor and wouldn't make that mistake again. Maka and I were great as a couple, and we both acknowledged that part of that was because we gave each other space. I didn't think that living together would change us or break us up, but I also wasn't quite ready for the change that would require.

I finished up my loco moco and cleared the table. Before I could begin washing the silverware, though, Maka reemerged from the bathroom, pulling his shirt back on over his head.

"That was fast," I remarked with a frown. "I didn't even hear you run any water."

"I'll have to shower later. Call Grace. I've got somewhere to take the two of you."

GRACE DROVE OVER to meet us, as confused as I was when she arrived. "What's going on? I was settling in to watch *Real Housewives*."

"I'll explain on the way. Let's get in the car."

Maka waited until we were on the road to fill us in. "I talked to one of my buddies in Missing Persons today after you guys left. Not 'Ōpūnui, but someone in the same department. From what I could gather, this is going just like a normal routine case, no reason to suspect that they're dragging their feet or not investigating fully."

"Okay, that doesn't explain where we're going."

Maka regarded Grace over his shoulder as he brought the car to a stop at a red light.

"Are you always this impatient?"

"Absolutely."

Maka waited for the light to turn green before continuing. "We're going to the airport. Or, more specifically, the airport parking garage."

"Seems like a pretty unusual place to take us," I said, confused. "Why?"

"Apparently a car has been in the parking garage for several days." I could already see where he was going with this, but let him finish. "One of the airport police ran the tag and it turns out the car belongs to Christine Hu, so they called Missing Persons. My buddy heard the call and gave me a heads up. I figured you two would like to see it before they tow it."

He was definitely right on that. "They're not going to let us do anything with the car, though, are they? Isn't it a crime scene or something?"

"They're probably not going to let you go crawling around, if that's what you mean, but you can at least listen in on their evaluation of it, ask questions, that sort of thing. *If* you're polite," he added with a pointed look Grace's direction.

"Why are you saying that to me?" Grace protested. "I'm *always* polite. I'm a goddamn ray of sunshine!"

"Tell that to Mrs. Neidermeyer," I sniggered.

"That is totally different. Unique circumstances are involved."

"Those unique circumstances being?"

"She started it!"

"What are you, twelve?" I taunted, earning a swift kick against the back of my seat.

"Hey!" Maka said sternly. "No kicking the seats."

Grace looked chagrined for all of a moment before she reached forward and pinched the back of my arm, just above my elbow.

Grace always fought dirty.

It was a bit of a drive to the airport from my place, and it took us nearly forty-five minutes to finally arrive. It took us another five minutes to find which parking garage the Missing Persons team was in, so by the time we arrived it looked like the crime scene techs were just about finished with their preliminary checks.

Standing in front of the car—a very new-looking Mercedes of some sort—clear of the path incoming and outgoing cars were taking, were Detective ʻŌpūnui and a guy who must have been his partner on the case—a willow-thin black guy who looked like a strong gust of wind would send him flying.

Maka parked his car on the other side of the car lane from where Christine's sat. When we exited the car ʻŌpūnui gave us a hard, long stare. I don't think he even blinked as we approached.

"What are you doing here, Kekoa?" ʻŌpūnui asked, his voice neutral. I wondered for the first time if bringing us here was going to get Maka in trouble. I hoped not; the last thing I wanted was for my job as a private detective to start complicating his work life. "Oh, and look, you've brought civilians. Sure the brass is just going to love this."

I did my best not to scowl at 'Ōpūnui, but I was starting to dislike him even more than Benet.

Maka seemed unperturbed by 'Ōpūnui's attitude. "They're here representing the girl's family, Rich. Got a problem with that?"

'Ōpūnui looked like he had a big problem with that, though if he did, he didn't say so. "What about you? Who are you here representing, Kekoa?"

Maka spread his arms widely. "No badge. I'm just here as a civilian to make sure these two don't do anything stupid." He ignored the daggers Grace glared his way.

"Well, you can take your civilians home, then. There's nothing for you to see here."

"Come on, Richard," Maka reasoned. "This is for the girl's mother. They aren't reporters, they're not going to run leaking information to the public before you're ready to make your ruling."

'Ōpūnui looked to his partner who gave a single nod. "Fine. I'll tell you what we know. The car has been here since the day the report says she went missing, according to the time stamp on the card in the window. There's no sign of forced entry, no indication it was hot-wired. CSI is going over it to see if there's any indication of blood or cleaner, but my guess is it's going to come up a big fat 'no.' All evidence that we've found supports the theory that she ran away with her personal assistant."

"A car being at an airport isn't exactly the most concrete proof," I said before I could think better of it. Maka sent me a mild look, eyebrow raised, but didn't look that angry. Maybe he was thinking the same thing?

"No, but we also have the fact that the personal assistant purchased two one-way tickets that day and withdrew a very large amount of money from his bank. And, coincidentally, Miss Hu also made a fairly large cash withdrawal from her account that afternoon. Based on phone records, it came right after a fight she had on the phone with her fiancé, Mr. Delgado. We've got no evidence to indicate she did anything other than leave. She'll probably be back after her fling with the assistant gets old."

"I'm sure that will be real comforting to her mother," Grace said quietly.

The look on 'Ōpūnui's face softened a bit. "You should go on and go home. Oh, and if you talk to Mrs. Hu before we do, let her know we'll be paying a visit."

'Ōpūnui turned his back on us, as clear a dismissal as you can get.

"Come on," Maka said, turning back to the car, Grace following. I stood there for a moment, though, wondering how it was that 'Ōpūnui could be so callous and flippant about something like that, so dismissive of the pain that Helena Hu must be feeling. I wanted him to look me in the eye just once before I left.

His back was still to me, and he was engaged in a conversation with his lanky partner. I didn't hear all of it, but I did catch a bit. "...up here..." Lanky's voice drifted to me. The sound of Maka or Grace's car door closing drowned out the first part of 'Ōpūnui's reply, but I did catch the end. "...Delgado a call."

That raised some eyebrows, figuratively and literally. So, 'Ōpūnui was going to give Delgado a call about what they found, but not Helena? That seemed iffy to me, and only made me more suspicious of Delgado's influence over the police.

"Gabe, let's go," Maka called from the car. I reluctantly turned away without meeting 'Ōpūnui's gaze and climbed into the car.

Grace caught my eyes in the sideview mirror, a question on her face. I just shook my head; I didn't want to talk about it in front of Maka. It wasn't that I didn't trust him, because I did, with my life. However, he was a police officer, and I doubted he'd be very receptive to any implication that there was corruption among his colleagues. It was hard to believe that people you thought you knew could be totally different than your perception.

It would be best for all of us if I kept Maka out of things as much as possible. I didn't want him to catch heat at work, and I definitely didn't want to put him in an awkward position.

No, this was up to me and Grace. I tried not to think about how much more difficult things would be if the police truly *were* working for Delgado.

THE NEXT MORNING was Saturday. I didn't always go into the office, but when we were working a case I often did. Grace and I had decided the night before, as I walked her to her car, that we definitely needed to get together the next day, given the revelations of the night.

Maka had the day off, so he was still asleep in my bed as I made my way toward the door. I'd made the mistake of hitting the snooze button instead of waking up—four times—and now I was running late.

I poured coffee in a thermos—no way I was drinking the stuff Grace made—and started out the door. It was still early, but it was a Saturday, which meant the roads would be packed with tourists and locals alike heading to the beaches or to enjoy the myriad of entertainment options Honolulu provided.

I'd just finished locking the door behind me—Maka would have lectured me if I didn't, even though there was, at that moment, a cop sleeping in my apartment—when the voice spoke up behind me.

"Excuse me?"

I nearly dropped my thermos but barely managed to hang on to it. That was a good thing, too; I loved that thermos, and it definitely would have shattered on the ground, leaving me with no coffee, and probably endangering the life of whoever had caused me to do that.

Standing directly behind me, far too close for my comfort, was a portly bald man with a huge bristling mustache that reminded me of an old walrus cartoon I used to see. He barely came up to my chest. He was dressed like a typical tourist, in a brightly colored Aloha print shirt and khaki cargo shorts. He carried a camera around his neck—a really expensive, high-powered one, by the looks of it.

"Who are you?" I demanded, taking a step back toward my door.

"You're Gabe Maxfield, yes?" The man's voice was overexcited. He used a cloth he kept in his pocket to mop the sweat from his shiny, bald head.

"I'm only going to say this one more time," I said firmly, dropping my free hand into my pocket to grab my keys. "Who are you?"

"We spoke yesterday," he said quickly, and just like that I recognized the voice.

"You're the paparazzi, right? Mr. Jackson."

"Jeffords, Braeden Jeffords. And it's paparazzo, actually. Paparazzi is plural." He extended his hand for me to shake, but I didn't take it.

"Are you stalking me, Mr. Jeffords?"

Braeden Jeffords looked positively terrified by the implication. "What? No! No, of course not."

"Really?" I was already running late and his interruption was just another annoyance I didn't need or want in my life right now, and I didn't bother to hide any of that in my voice. "First you call me on my private cell phone, and now you're turning up at my home? Sounds like stalking to me. Besides, aren't you a professional stalker?"

"I'm a photographer," Jeffords stammered. "And if you'd just hear me out—"

"Mr. Jeffords, I'm going to stop you right there. I'm not interested in whatever it is you have to say. I'm extremely busy and this has been very inconvenient. You probably know that my boyfriend is a cop. Well, he's right inside as we speak, so if you don't turn around and go back wherever it is you came from in the next twenty seconds, I'm going to have to go wake him up, and he's even worse than me in the mornings."

"But I can help you," he said anxiously.

"I'm not currently in need of a paparazzo today, thanks," I said as sarcastically as I could. "And fourteen seconds."

Jeffords released a huff through his nose, making his mustache flare out. If there was one thing that could be said for Mr. Braeden Jeffords, though, it was that he was smart enough to guess that I wasn't kidding because he didn't try to call my bluff. He just scooted off back to his car. I made careful note of it in case he tried to follow me.

I didn't trust his story, that he was paparazzi. I thought it far more likely that he worked for Delgado and was keeping an eye on me, like those two men I'd seen the night before.

I wondered for a moment if I was doing the right thing, not telling Maka about them, especially after this run-in with Jeffords. If Maka found out about it, he would probably be furious with me. On the other hand, this was my job and I'd come to accept it, just like I accepted that there was danger involved in his. Granted, there probably shouldn't be quite as much danger in mine as there had been, but that wasn't my fault.

Well, the first time was. The second time was all on Grace.

I was surprised to find that Mrs. Neidermeyer was at work when I got there. I didn't expect her to come in on a Saturday. At least today she was wearing something appropriate. Well, more appropriate than usual, anyway.

"What are you doing here, Mrs. Neidermeyer?"

"You two are working a case, aren't you?" she said, as if that explained everything.

"True," I allowed, "but it's Saturday. And your ankle."

"You two are useless without me, and you know it. Besides, my ankle's fine. Going to take more than a bad dismount from a stripper pole in heels to bring me down." She propped her feet up on the desk and pulled a large print library edition of *Fifty Shades of Grey* from her purse.

Questionable reading habits aside, I decided to just leave her be. Before I could go into the back Grace emerged. She raised an eyebrow and looked at her watch meaningfully and I just shrugged in return.

"Mrs. Neidermeyer," Grace said slowly, tilting her head so she could see the cover of the old woman's book. "Are you reading *Fifty Shades of Gray*?"

"Yes. I can't figure out why this book is considered so erotic? It's just got spanking in it. I guess I've been erotic since nineteen thirty-three."

Grace and I shared a shuddering look. "On that note, I think we've got work to do."

We went back into Grace's office and closed the door behind us. "Well," she said, sounding defeated, "I'm not sure where we go from here. The police have it wrapped up in a nice bow, and all the evidence points to their findings."

"Conveniently," I added. I told her what I overheard the previous night, the two men I saw, and about Braeden Jeffords. "It just sounds like Manny Delgado has his fingers all over this. I'm not sure we can trust the police on this one."

Grace looked shaken. "Have you talked about this theory with Maka?"

"What? No. How on earth can I tell him that I think that some of his colleagues are dirty? That's the last thing I need."

"He knows that dirty cops exist," Grace reasoned.

"Knowing they exist and knowing that someone in your precinct is one are two different things." I shook my head. "I'd rather not go to him with this being just a theory. If we have hard evidence, then I'll go to him. Until then, it's you and me."

Grace smiled. "Just the way we like it, right?"

I sat down in the chair across from her, removed my shoes, and drew my knees to my chest, heels on the edge of the chair. "Actually, I had an idea last night on how we might manage to get a lead."

Grace propped her elbows on her desk and her chin on her fist dramatically. "Go on."

"Well, we have evidence that Christine talked to Sergio at the time he said, right? We can't assume to know what they talked about, but we know a conversation took place. Then we have her car arriving at the airport. We know it happened that day but not *when*. We need to establish some sort of a timeline for her if we want to get a good idea of what happened."

"Okay, but the woman in question is missing, so how do you recommend we do that, Sherlock?"

I made a face. "What, that makes you Watson? You, my dear, are no Lucy Liu."

"Ouch. That hurts my feelings," Grace said, deadpan. "Now, what's this idea of yours?"

I grinned. "I think you're going to like this idea. We call Jin Hamada."

Chapter Six

I HADN'T SEEN Grace look as nervous as she did at that moment in a long time. It was off-putting. I was so used to a Grace who was comfortable, strong in her power, not this mass of awkward anxiety I saw before me.

We were waiting in the front office for Jin to show up. The two of us were sitting on the couch there for waiting clients, Mrs. Neidermeyer still engrossed in her book.

Grace shifted around like there were ants crawling all over her. She would cross her leg one way and then immediately switch and cross it the other way.

"Would you sit still?" I admonished. "What has gotten into you?"

"It's who she *wants* to get in her," Mrs. Neidermeyer piped up, not looking away from her book.

"Mrs. Neidermeyer, please refrain from talking about my sex life," Grace groaned.

Mrs. Neidermeyer finally lowered her book. "How is it a woman with those hips and that chest can be such a prude?"

Grace stiffened, mouth forming an outraged 'O'. "I am *not* a prude! I'd just prefer not to talk about my sex life with someone older than my grandmother!"

"You think I haven't had sex before, Grace Park?"

I could barely choke back my laugh, though I managed to turn it into a cough. I doubt Grace was fooled, though, based on her glare.

"No amount of therapy will ever help me unhear this conversation."

Grace was still blushing beneath her sun-kissed skin when Jin showed up. He was just a bit shorter than me with long hair. When I'd first met him, the lower portion had been dyed bright blue, but that was gone and now acid green streaks replaced it. He had triple piercings in his ears and an affinity for band t-shirts. That day he wore one for Babymetal, a Japanese female heavy metal band. The barest flashes of his incomplete tattoo sleeve peeked out from under the sleeve of his T-shirt.

"Morning, everyone," he said in his usual cheerful way. He produced a box of donuts. "I brought donuts for the class."

"You're an angel, Jin Hamada," Mrs. Neidermeyer said, clearing a space on her desk for the box.

"It's no problem, not for my favorite clients." He flashed a dazzling smile at us.

"Hear that, Grace?" Mrs. Neidermeyer snickered. "He said we're his favorite clients."

Grace looked like she wanted to jump across the desk and put her hands over Mrs. Neidermeyer's mouth, but she restrained herself.

We helped ourselves to donuts and then led Jin back to Grace's office. "Thanks for coming by on such short notice," I said, moving a chair out for Jin.

"No problem," Jin managed around a mouthful of donut. "When you guys said you'd be willing to pay my Sunday rates I knew it was important."

"It is, I think. But actually, first Grace wanted to ask you something." I gave her an encouraging nod. "Right, Grace?"

"What? I don't know..." I couldn't believe my ears. Where had the confident and powerful Grace Park gone? How had she gotten replaced with the woman sitting with me, who kept her eyes on the surface of her desk, not risking a look in Jin's direction.

"Grace," I prompted through clenched teeth. I wished the desk didn't have that barrier between us so I could kick her in hopes of getting her out of whatever this phase was.

"Well, tomorrow night there's going to be a dinner—at Maka's house—not a big thing, just a few of us, you know, nothing fancy or anything like that." I could tell by the look on Grace's face that she knew that she was babbling but just didn't know how to stop it. "Anyway, would, uh, would you like to come?"

"Tomorrow? Sure, sounds fun."

"Great!" I cringed as Grace's voice rose two octaves. "I'll text you how to get to Maka's place later. Great. This will be fun—like, really fun. I'm excited."

Oh, Grace. "So, on to business," I interjected, trying to spare her more humiliation. "The reason we called you here is because we wanted to ask your help on a case."

Jin nodded. "Yeah, I figured. What's the case?"

I filled him in on everything. "So I was hoping we could fill in the gaps using her car GPS system. Is there any way you could do that?"

Jin shrugged. "Yeah. There's two ways. If the data is still there, then we just need to look at previous locations. If not, it's a bit trickier, and not technically legal, but I can get the information from the company's database itself."

"Great," I said, getting to my feet. "Now we need to call Helena and see if she can get us access to the car."

"I'll do it," Grace said quickly, digging through the paperwork to find Helena's number. The conversation they had was short and to the point; Grace explained what we wanted to do, listened for a moment, said thank you, and then hung up.

"Okay, she said she'll arrange to have the car at her place, the address we have on the form. So we just have to meet her there. You two should go quickly."

I blinked. "You should go, don't you think? Or all of us together, yeah?" I couldn't understand why she was passing up an opportunity to go with Jin herself.

"No, I've got some paperwork to finish filing to get off on the Amberhill case. You two go on and take care of that." She passed me the form with Helena Hu's address on it. "Here you go."

I took the paper and then caught her eyes, trying to figure out what was going through her head, but she looked away quickly, either too ashamed or not wanting to deal with it.

"Okay," I said, casting one last dubious look her way before turning to Jin. "Let's go."

HELENA HU LIVED out in Diamond Head, one of the wealthiest neighborhoods not just in Honolulu but on all of Oahu. It was still pretty early in the day, not yet ten, so I hoped traffic wouldn't be too bad.

Jin grabbed a laptop case from his car and got in the passenger seat of my car—it made more sense, since I could charge the cost of gas to Helena as a business expense.

The sky was overcast, promising rain, which kept the glare of the sun minimal as I drove east.

Up to that point I hadn't spent much time alone with Jin; Jin and I had developed a friendship, but it had been one based on the orbits of others in our lives—usually if we were together then Grace or Maka or someone else was with us as well.

I liked Jin. He was an easygoing guy with a fun personality who had a way of making everyone feel at ease around him, including me.

I still couldn't figure out why Grace had passed the opportunity to spend this time with Jin. Had all of her recent inability to communicate herself, the failed attempts at courtship, completely sapped her of her confidence?

"You know, Jin," I said, deciding to take advantage of the situation to do some work for Grace. "I was just thinking that we haven't ever had any heart to heart chats."

"Yeah," said Jin easily enough. "I guess that's true."

"Do you have a girlfriend?" I cringed at the question, wondering if it was too obvious as to why I was asking.

Jin cast me a playful look. "Nah, I'm single, but I'm pretty sure you're not, right?"

I snorted. "Darn, I was hoping that little fact would have escaped you. You've seen through my plan, Hamada."

"I've been single for a while now," he added. "Last long-term relationship was about three years ago. I've met people since then, mostly girls from Tinder or dudes from Unzipped, but those were usually one-date things. None of them caught my interest, or else they weren't looking for what I'm looking for."

For a moment my mind caught on the revelation that Jin was bi— well, not so much on the fact that he was, because that wasn't my business, but how casually he mentioned it—considering we hadn't had lots of one-on-one time.

"I can't imagine Unzipped produces lots of relationship-minded guys," I managed.

"Actually," he chuckled, "a lot of times it was the girls that seemed thirstier."

We shared a deep belly laugh then.

"When did you start working for Paradise Investigations?" I asked once the laughter had subsided, navigating my way toward the exit for Diamond Head.

"Two years ago. Grace contacted me about working for them on a case where relevant information regarding a contested will was trapped on the computer of the deceased and no one could access it. After that case, I offered to make myself available if they needed me again, and they've—no, you've—kept me frequently employed."

I contemplated the best way to talk to him about Grace without being too overt and clueing him off to what I'm doing without knowing how he would feel about it. I decided the best tactic would be to make jokes.

"Do you always hang out with your employers?"

Jin grinned. "Only when they're as cool as Grace."

"Did you spend much time with Carrie outside of work?"

"Not really. Carrie was..." He spent a moment searching for a word, settling on: "driven. I respected the hell out of it. The woman had goals, and she did what it took to make it happen. That didn't leave a lot of time for fun and hanging out. Grace, though, she's always been fun."

Was there something in his voice when he said that, or was it just my imagination?

The navigation system in my car spoke up then, telling me to take the upcoming left turn.

"These are some fancy houses," Jin commented, and he was understating it. Diamond Head Road was approaching us, and the houses were various sizes and styles, but they were all opulent in their own way. The houses appeared to be built in different time periods, including some early colonial plantations right beside sprawling modern day mansions.

"Right? Wish I had the money to live in one of these."

"Don't you?" Jin prompted. He'd heard Grace tease me about being a trust fund kid on several occasions.

"I guess technically, but I can't access enough of it at a time to buy a house. And I'd only be able to stay in one a month before it was foreclosed."

Jin grinned. "It would be a nice month, though."

He had a valid point.

Conversation died out as the navigation began talking more frequently, navigating us to Helena Hu's house.

Her home was more subdued than some of the others, but it was still large and grand. The lawn was perfectly trimmed, a small fountain in the front halfway between the driveway and the front porch.

Two cars were in the driveway, one of them the car the police had been crawling over the night before. I was impressed that she had access to it already. I figured it would have taken more time for the police to process it. No doubt money at work.

"Is that the client?" Jin asked, nodding his head toward the porch. "'Cause she looks mad."

I brought the car to a stop behind Christine's car and looked where Jin indicated. Helena Hu stood there on the porch, her arms crossed over her chest, something tucked under her arm. Jin was right; her face was set, her eyes seemed to blaze with bright fire. She was dressed in just a simple white blouse that draped her body, and nice, simple jeans.

"Yeah, that's her, and yeah she looks mad. This ought to be fun."

As Jin and I exited the car Helena came charging down the steps and across the cobblestone walkway that made its way past the fountain to where we were.

"I can't believe those incompetent police officers! They spend more time looking for missing cats! And look at this!" She practically threw what she was holding at me. It was a newspaper, the metro section, the front page with the headline *Heiress Runs Off with Assistant*. "The same morning they call to tell me about their findings this story was in the paper. Tell me how a reporter found all of this out before I did?"

"That's, uh," I stammered, but Helena had no intention of letting me speak.

"This is just to spin the court of public opinion their way so that there's no pressure to finish the investigation," she went on, practically smoking.

"It's not going to deter Grace and me, Mrs. Hu," I assured her. "That's why we're here. This is Jin Hamada. He's our tech expert. We hire him to handle the technical aspects of cases. He's helped us out countless times."

"Pleasure to meet you," Helena said, taking Jin's hand, the anger slowly fading from her voice. "What are you going to do exactly?"

"Establish a timeline, if we can," I explained. "We have the police information about the time that she made the phone call to Sergio, but we don't know what happened after that. I'm hoping that Mr. Hamada here can give us a better idea of that."

Helena reached into her pocket and pulled out a car key. "I had the spare," she said, suddenly melancholy. "I have the spares of all of her keys."

I took the key from her and unlocked the car door, holding it open for Jin to look in and see what they were dealing with. He muttered something to himself that I didn't hear and then held his hand out for the key.

With it he started the car and keyed up the GPS system.

Helena came and stood next to me as we both watched Jin work.

"Someone deleted the history," Jin announced after a moment.

"So we're nowhere?" I asked, frowning.

"Not exactly. It would have been easiest to just get it right off the device's built in history, but that's not the only place it is. The data still exists in the company's database. Now, most GPS companies won't release that information without a warrant—"

"Which we can't get since the investigation is officially closed," Helena said sourly.

"We might not need one," I assured her. "Jin, can you work around this?"

"I'm pretty sure I can, yeah." Jin emerged from the car and went back to mine, bringing out his laptop bag. He unpacked his laptop and plugged in a USB cord to it. At the other end of the cord was another USB plug, which he plugged into the USB slot on the bottom of the GPS.

Helena looked at me over the top of the car. "I'm going to take a wild guess and say that none of this is legal."

"Would you rather we stopped?"

"Hell no. Whatever it takes to find my daughter. I'll take care of any legal bills that might arise."

"Okay." Jin disconnected the USB cable and closed his laptop up. "I've got what I need to get to work on this. It might take a little bit of time."

"I'm grateful for anything you can do."

"Mrs. Hu, I've got one more question. What was the name of the company that your daughter found Travis Brent through?"

"Halimer and Gold," Helena answered immediately. "Sounds like a law firm, right? But they handle personal assistants for lots of important people not just here but all over Hawai'i and even on the mainland, too."

A quick Google search showed me what I needed to know. "Looks like their office is on the way back to Paradise Investigations. Jin, what do you say we stop by and see if anyone is there who can talk to us. Google says they're open Monday through Saturday, so *someone* should be."

"Last time I did any of the actual investigative work with you I nearly got shot," he said dubiously.

"This is a white-collar office building, Jin. The worst that can happen is someone throws a stapler at you."

"Okay, fine. But I'm hiding behind you if staplers *do* go flying."

"What are the chances of that actually happening?"

"With *you*? Probably pretty high."

AS MUCH AS the name resembled a law firm, the building housing Halimer and Gold did as well. I honestly would have assumed them to just be a high-profile group, probably one that practiced corporate law or focused on taking down big business, like the law firm where I was once a paralegal—Hampton, Wyler, Morgan and Rodriguez.

"This is a really fancy place," Jin commented, looking around. "How much do you think these PAs charge by the hour?"

"Probably way more than either of us can afford."

There was a security guard at the front desk, and she got up the moment we came in. She looked none too pleased to be working on Saturday, and I hoped we didn't take the brunt of her ire.

When she spoke, her voice was pleasant enough, a rich alto that made me really want to hear her sing. "How can I help you gentlemen today?"

"We're here to talk to someone from Halimer and Gold," I said as kindly as I could.

She studied us for a moment, looking us over from head to toe, before saying, "Okay. Fourth floor."

Jin waited until the elevator doors closed before saying, "Well, that was easier than I thought it would be. I figured they'd ask if we had an appointment or something."

"That'll probably happen when we go into the Halimer and Gold office, don't worry."

The elevator reached the fourth floor and opened into a very *white* lobby. The furniture was cream colored, the walls, eggshell white, and the floor, glistening marble. Even the counter was white. The biggest splash of color was the secretary's crimson red blouse and the gold lettering of the company's name on the wall directly behind her.

"Welcome to Halimer and Gold," the woman said cheerfully, her brightly red-painted lips spreading into a wide and genuinely friendly smile. "How may I help you?"

I cleared my throat and adopted the voice I used to try to sound professional, what Grace called my Mr. Business Voice. "I'm Gabe

Maxfield, this is my associate Jin Hamada. We're from Paradise Investigations." I presented my card to her. She bore a name badge that read "Jennifer."

The friendly smile faltered somewhat when she saw I was a private investigator. "What is this about?"

"We've been hired by Helena Hu, the mother of Christine Hu, to find out some information about what happened to her daughter."

At the mention of Christine's name, Jennifer's face soured. "You want to ask questions about Travis."

So, she knows him. "That's right. Do you know who could best answer those questions?"

"I think pretty much anyone here could, but if you're asking who he reported to, it would be Shonda Wilks."

"Is she in?"

Jennifer shook her head. "No, I'm afraid not. She only works Tuesday through Friday. I can call her in, if you want, but I don't know if she'll answer or be able to come in."

"If you could try, that would be nice."

Jin and I waited. Jin leaned over to me and whispered, "I'm pretty sure she knows the guy."

I nodded. "I thought so too. We definitely need to ask her some questions."

"I'm sorry," Jennifer said, hanging up the phone. "Shonda can't make it in today. She's on the Big Island visiting her parents. The earliest she can come in is Tuesday, on her normal work shift."

"Oh, we understand," I said quickly. I didn't think that Shonda would be the more beneficial one to talk to, after all, so I wasn't too disappointed. "Did you know Travis Brent?"

"Yes," she said. She blushed, for some reason, and added, "I mean, we all did. I know we seem like a big company, but everyone knows everyone here. We have lots of company bonding activities."

The corner of Jin's lips turned up and I could read his thoughts pretty clearly in his eyes, because I was certain they mirrored my own. She'd definitely been involved in "bonding activities" with Travis.

"Can you tell us a little about him?"

"He was a great guy. Friendly, sweet. He looked out for everybody. He was great at his job, too. I don't think we had a more professional employee here."

I raised an eyebrow. "Oh really? From what I heard—"

"Those are all lies," Jennifer interrupted. "Travis would have never done anything with that Christine Hu."

"You sound pretty certain of that," Jin remarked.

Jennifer's face flushed darker. "We have a strict company policy. No fraternizing of any kind with employers. No friendship, nothing...else, either."

"People break employee policy all the time," I said casually. "Right?"

"Not Travis," Jennifer repeated firmly. "Not Travis. Not with Christine." She clamped her mouth shut, then, like she'd said too much.

"Not with *Christine*," Jin repeated shrewdly. "Does that mean he would with someone else?"

Jennifer looked around to make sure no other employees were around. "Yes. Travis and I were a thing."

"How long has that been going on?" Jin asked the question the way a friend might, not like he was interrogating her for information. I couldn't help but think that he was really good at this. If his tech career went down the drain, he could always have a backup as a private investigator. I know I'd hire him on the spot, and I was pretty sure that Grace would too.

"Three months. It started as a casual dinner and went from there. And I can tell you without a doubt that he wasn't sleeping with Christine Hu. I kept him plenty satisfied."

"I'm sure, I'm sure."

I was impressed by this new side of Jin I was seeing. The man was smooth—he had game, or whatever the expression was. How on earth he was still single was beyond me.

"He looked at Christine Hu as a normal employer. A *boring* one at that. She didn't do much but organize gala events for her mother's charity. It wasn't until she got engaged that Travis actually felt like he was working."

"How did Travis feel about the engagement?" I asked.

"I don't know that he had an opinion on it either way. It wasn't something for him to have anything to say about, you know? He didn't get involved in any of his clients' personal lives. He didn't even know when her birthday was."

I nodded, doing my best to remember all of that, wishing I'd brought my notepad with me. "I have one last question. Were you and Travis serious?"

Jennifer took several deep breaths before answering. "Honestly? I was starting to fall in love with him. I thought he felt the same way about me."

"Did you know that Travis purchased one-way plane tickets and withdrew a lot of money from his bank account the day that Christine Hu went missing?"

"They," Jennifer said, her voice tinny.

I frowned. "Excuse me?"

"The day *they* went missing, Mr. Maxfield. Travis is also missing, not just Christine, but I don't see a lot of fancy private investigators going around trying to find him."

"Hopefully we'll find both of them. But I really need you to answer the question. Did you know—"

"About the plane tickets? No. Not until the police asked me about them in the initial interview. I don't have any explanation for that."

"Thank you for your time," I said gently, leaving my card with her.

Jin and I drove back to Paradise Investigations. I figured that Grace was probably going crazy, wondering when or if we were coming back. I idly wondered if she'd killed Mrs. Neidermeyer yet.

But Mrs. Neidermeyer was alive and well when we returned to Paradise Investigations, though judging from the irate expression on Grace's face, we'd arrived just in the nick of time.

"Where have you been?" I would have had flashbacks to an overbearing mother if I'd had an overbearing mother.

"Doing my job," I replied, flopping down on the couch. "Jin and I picked up a lead and went to talk to them on the way back."

As she listened to my rundown of the meeting with both Helena and Jennifer, Grace nodded. "That syncs with what I'd heard, too." Off of my surprised look she made a face. "You're not the only one who can track down leads alone. I finished up paperwork and called the top three people on the list of Christine's friends. They didn't say much—just that there was no way that Christine and Travis had a thing going. They've agreed to sit down and talk with us Monday afternoon."

"Does that mean we're all done here?" Mrs. Neidermeyer asked, packing up her book. "I've got somewhere to be."

"Not your stripper classes, I hope," Grace muttered loud enough for everyone to hear.

"Pole dancing is Thursday night," Mrs. Neidermeyer replied primly. "Tonight I've got a date. With a younger man, I might add."

"A younger man, huh?"

"You know it, kiddo." Mrs. Neidermeyer patted my cheek playfully as she walked by me on her way out the door.

"Got to give her props," Jin said when she was gone. "I hope I'm still sexually active when I'm her age."

I stood up quickly. "Wow. On that note, I think it's time to head home."

Jin hoisted his laptop bag onto his shoulder. "I'll get started on tracing her steps. See you tomorrow."

"Tomorrow?" Grace repeated faintly.

"The dinner party. Remember?"

"Oh, right, yeah." Grace ran a hand through her hair. "I totally—just—yeah, slipped my mind."

She crashes and burns saying goodbye. It was one of the most cringeworthy things I'd seen in a while. I felt badly for Grace, but there wasn't anything I could do to help her, not right then.

The awkwardness came to an end, finally, with Jin's departure. As soon as he was gone Grace turned to me, throwing her arms around me, moaning. "That was a disaster."

"It could have been worse," I comforted, though I was hard pressed to think of how.

"It could?"

I knew you were going to ask me that. "Sure it could. Uh...oh! Mrs. Neidermeyer could have seen that."

Grace was silent for a beat. "I feel better now."

Chapter Seven

BY ELEVEN SUNDAY morning, I was in Maka's kitchen helping him clean fish. He'd been to the fish market early that morning and bought two big ahi tuna. As we went, Maka taught me about the dish he was making.

"*Poke* is served with a lot of different seafood—crab or salmon, for example—but it's most traditionally served with ahi tuna."

"*Poke* is sushi, right? That's what it means?" I had just about finished descaling one side of my ahi.

"No. *Poke* means to cut. It refers to the style of preparation of the food. The raw fish is a major influence of the island's Japanese heritage as well." He shot me a sheepish look. "If you want me to stop lecturing now, I will."

"What? No! I love when you teach me things about Hawai'ian culture," I assured him. "I'm lucky to have you. I'd still be like a dumb tourist if you hadn't taken me under your wing."

He grinned, leaning over to capture my lips in a quick, chaste kiss. "We'll have you living like a local in no time, don't worry."

Maka turned his attention to the fish in my hand and laughed. "Okay, give me the fish."

I handed the tuna over to him, chagrined. "I didn't grow up around fish," I explained.

Maka did his best to keep a straight face. "I can tell."

I wasn't offended by his observation; I knew I wasn't doing a great job descaling it, whereas Maka had sped through his like he'd been born to it.

"How old were you when you started helping cook the fish?" I asked, putting the descaler down in the sink and washing my hands quickly. I knew I wouldn't be able to get rid of the smell of the fish so easily, but I could certainly try.

"It's a big deal in a Hawaiian family," he explained, not missing a beat with his descaler. "I mean, most meals are. Everybody helps in some way. When I turned ten, I started helping my father and uncles descale the fish. Before then I helped make the rice. My sister always got to marinate the fish once it was cut, which made me mad. She always had the easier job."

"Well, it's a good thing I'm not the one in charge of the meal," I joked.

"I'm not going to agree or disagree with that, in case it's a trap."

"You're on to my games, I see."

There were other things I could do in the kitchen, while Maka began to cut the fish into one-inch cubes. I was more than happy being Maka's prep chef. I cut sweet onion into thin slices, minced garlic, and cut shallots on a bias. I would have all the prep work done when he finished his task.

I watched him work, just enjoying the whole scenario. It was straight out of my childhood and teenage daydreams, the way this was. Maka there in a T-shirt with his old high school logo on it and a pair of mesh basketball shorts, apron covering it, focused on some task in his kitchen. I felt content, in that moment, utterly at peace with the choices in my life that led me to where I was.

"You're putting a lot of energy into this dinner party," I observed, leaning against the counter between Maka and the refrigerator. He'd finished cubing the fish and had thrown it into a glass bowl.

"Well, it's happening, so I'm not going to do it half-assed, you know?"

"You know what I mean," I pressed. "We're having this party specifically for Grace and Jin. That seems like a lot."

"It's not specifically for Grace and Jin, that's just...icing on the cake." He liberally added olive oil to the fish until it was all but glistening in the kitchen light.

"Why do you care so much about the two of them, though?"

"Grace is your friend," Maka said, like that was the only answer I needed—and maybe it was. "She's my friend, too, and so is Jin. I want them to be happy. I feel sorry for Grace when she's around us. I mean, we found each other, and we're happy. Think about it—we're lucky. I just feel bad for Grace when she has to be around us so much. It has to make her lonely."

I slipped my arms around his waist, resting my forehead against the space between his shoulder blades. "You're such a great guy."

"Yeah, I know," he said, and I could hear his grin in his voice. "Bring me the seasonings."

I released him and brought over two containers of things I didn't recognize. One was black and reminded me of darker sesame seeds, the other red. "What are these?" I asked.

"This," he picked up the red seasoning, "is *'alaea*. It's salt mixed with volcanic clay. It's got a real earthy taste, more than a salty one."

He liberally added it to the fish. Next, he took the ingredients I'd already chopped and added them to the fish, using his hands to mix them all together.

Finally, he took up the black seasoning I didn't recognize. "And this is *inamona*. I don't know what you'd call it on the mainland. It's made with *kukui* nuts." He gave me a questioning look and I shrugged. I had no idea what a *kukui* nut was.

He added the *inamona* and mixed it again. When he finished, he washed his hands. "Can you cover the bowl with plastic wrap and put it in the refrigerator?"

I did as he asked, making sure the *poke* was well covered and placing it on the spot he'd cleared just for it.

"That needs to chill in there for at least two hours," he said as he dried his hands. "The rice will need to start cooking in about two hours, too. That gives us plenty of time."

I perked up at the implication of that. I liked where he was going with this. I gave him my most suggestive look. "Oh? Time for what?"

He slinked up to me, wrapping his arms around me, one hand sliding up to the back of my neck, the other sliding down to the curve of my ass. He kissed me again, and there was nothing chaste about this one. It left my breath short and my pants feeling particularly tight.

Maka brought his lips against my ear and whispered, "To clean."

MAKA WAS SERIOUS about that, too. We cleaned every nook and cranny. I was grateful, though, that Maka decided to clean the bathroom and let me clean the living room. Sure, it was more space for me to clean, but I hated the smell of bleach and other chemicals necessary to clean the bathroom. I hated doing it in my own place, and I would much rather avoid doing it at someone else's.

Even if that someone else *was* Maka.

By the time we finished cleaning, it was right about time for the guests to begin to arrive.

I thought that, given the circumstances, Grace would be the first to show up, but she wasn't. Hiapo arrived with a big handle of clear alcohol in either hand.

I grimaced at the sight of the bottles. "Please tell me that's not *okolehao*." I'd had run-ins with the traditional Hawaiian alcohol before, and they'd led to some pretty embarrassing memories for me—including me trying to bring a cooked pig head home with me in Maka's car.

"I can't lie to you, Gabe, so I just won't answer the question." Hiapo walked past me, handing the bottles to Maka. I glared at Maka, who just shrugged. "I figured the *okolehao* would maybe help Grace and Jin loosen up."

I thought about it for a minute. Given Grace's behavior recently it might not be such a bad idea. "Well, when you put it that way, I don't see what it can hurt." It would be good to see Grace get some of her old confidence back. I guess anybody could lose their groove, if they struck out enough times.

I stood awkwardly by the door, waiting for Grace to show up. I really hoped she would be there in time for me to talk her up a bit, get her feeling like the old Grace. It had reached the point where I was starting to wonder if she was going to come at all.

I was just taking my phone out to call her when the doorbell rang. Figuring it was her, I ended the call and opened the door. Thankfully, it was Grace, though I was less thankful about the outfit she was in.

"I made it." She smiled at me nervously. "Is Jin here yet, or did I beat him?"

"You beat him," I said, stepping aside to let her in. Maka must have heard her voice, because he came into the room from the back.

"Grace, you made...it." His eyes widened in an expression I could only assume mirrored my own when he took in Grace. She wore a red cocktail dress, one that fit her form flawlessly and would not have looked out of place at an extremely upscale or expensive bar. "We were beginning to wonder what had happened to you."

"I couldn't decide on what to wear," she said self-consciously.

"I see you decided," I said. I tried to keep my voice neutral, but she picked up on my tone right away.

"It's too much, isn't it? See, I knew it would be. I thought it showed off my body well—"

"It definitely does that," I interrupted.

"—but I just look like an overdressed idiot." Panic settled on her face, her eyes bugging a bit. "Jin is going to see me and think I'm a total idiot."

"No," I said, though I wanted to agree with her. "I'm pretty sure you've got some clothes at my place. Why don't you go over and see if you can find something that doesn't look like you're dressed to go to the Grammys before he gets here?"

"Okay. Okay, good idea."

Grace took my key and opened the front door only to come face to face with Jin, his finger poised just over the doorbell button. He could have caught flies in his mouth, the way he gaped at Grace. I saw his eyes do the sweep from head to toe—lingering on her breasts several seconds both times.

"Am I...am I underdressed?" He examined his own clothes—a solid blue short-sleeve button-down over a white T-shirt and a pair of dark pants.

"Uh, no, you're not," I said quickly, coming up beside Grace. "Grace here just always dresses to impress."

Grace just smiled, though I could tell she was quietly panicking inside that head of hers. "Grace and I were actually going to go next door to get something really fast," I went on, taking her by the elbow. "Go on in, make yourself comfortable. We'll be right back."

Once Jin closed the door behind him, I led Grace to my front door. There was nothing inside to get, and I figured there would be as good a place as any to have a conversation. "Girl, I need you to get it together! What is going on with you?"

"I wish I knew," Grace answered. "Honestly, I've just become so convinced that I'm going to screw up that I, you know, screw up. It's this whole awful self-fulfilling prophecy, and the more I do it the easier it gets."

"Where's the Grace I knew in college? The Grace who would march right up to a guy and tell him that he was taking her out?"

Grace shrugged. "She grew up into me. I haven't liked a guy in a long time. Those boys in college, they were easy. They were just fun, meant to occupy my time. Entertainment, that's it. I'm at the point where I'm looking for more than just entertainment, and I really think Jin has the potential to be exactly what I want in that department. It's a bit intimidating."

"Just be yourself. Don't get in your head. It's just a calm, casual dinner with friends. Nothing else."

"Right. That's it. I got this."

"Damn right you do!"

As we walked back into the apartment, Maka and Jin were emerging from the back. "Dude, Gabe, Maka just showed me the sweet board you got him for Christmas."

I blushed a little. "Well, it was my fault his board broke, so I had to replace it."

Jin raised an eyebrow. "How'd that happen?"

"I don't want to talk about it," I said, blushing.

"Grace likes telling this story," Maka said, and I groaned.

"It *is* a good one," Grace conceded, patting my shoulder apologetically. "We were getting ready to go out for a surfing lesson in my Jeep. It was good weather, so I had it open. It was Gabe's job to secure the boards so they didn't go flying. He did a crappy job—sorry, Gabe, but you did—and we hadn't gotten more than a mile before the rope came undone and Maka's surfboard slid right out of the Jeep and into the street. Got run over by not one but *two* cars before we could get it back."

"I thought they were secure," I grumbled. "And that's why I bought him the new one. I told them me taking up surfing was a terrible idea."

"Do you surf, Jin?" Maka asked, directing the attention directly away from me, thankfully.

"A little bit. I've done it before, but never been that good at it. I've thought about doing it, but I'd make a fool of myself."

I snorted. "I know exactly what you mean there."

Maka swatted at me playfully. "You want to go make sure the rice is ready?"

"Not really," I said even as I made my way into the kitchen. Hiapo had already taken care of the rice, portioning out five bowls to serve as the base of the *poke*. "See, Hiapo's got this. I trust him *way* more than I'd trust myself when it comes to cooking."

Hiapo gave me an appreciative nod.

"You know," Maka said, ignoring me. "Grace is a really good teacher. She's got Gabe surfing, so she can definitely get you up to snuff."

"I don't like being your examples," I called to them, knowing they would ignore me. I got the *poke* out of the refrigerator and passed it to Hiapo.

"I don't think I should take credit for it," Grace said quickly, and she was right, I thought. She was my best friend, and I loved her, but she didn't have a lot of patience—at least she didn't with me. The minor increase in my surfing abilities—that being my ability to actually stand on a surfboard without immediately falling over—was attributed entirely to Maka's way more patient and more reward-driven style of teaching.

Not that I was going to say that to Jin.

"Maybe I could head out with you guys one day, get some pointers," Jin suggested, smiling toward Grace.

"I'll uh, I'll do my best," Grace said with a similar smile.

"Who wants okolehao with their *poke*?" Hiapo asked loudly, popping the top off of one of the bottles.

"I'm driving," Jin and Grace both said quickly, sharing amused looks.

"Me too," Hiapo said with a frown. "So, looks like I'm camping out on your floor tonight, Maka."

"Or you could just not drink," Maka suggested, hurrying into the kitchen and taking the open bottle from the bigger man.

"I guess that means more for you and Gabe," Hiapo said.

"Yay," I said, unable to hide my lack of enthusiasm. I couldn't leave Maka to drink it all alone, though, so I accepted a glass. Maka knew my taste very well, and poured a liberal amount of pineapple Fanta into mine to help disguise the god-forsaken burn of the potent moonshine.

"It looks great, Maka," Jin said, taking in the bowl in front of him.

He wasn't wrong; I'd been worried that just the *poke* alone wouldn't be enough, but seeing it there in the bowls on top of the rice I realized I shouldn't have been. Maka's judgment was sound, as always.

"This is going to be delicious," I said, giving Maka a smile as I lifted my fork.

"I hope so. Everybody dig in."

No more than five minutes into the meal, there came a knock at the door. I tensed, looking toward Maka to see if he was expecting anyone else. He'd only set out enough places for the five of us, though, so I assumed he wasn't.

Maka put down his fork and went to the door. I was sitting with my back to the front door so I had to twist around in my chair to see, but I couldn't see the door itself, though I could see Maka's surprise.

"Can I help you?"

"Is this the home of Maka Kekoa?"

It was a man's voice that answered, and hearing it transported me right back to when I was a child. The same stern tone, the same crisp inflection combined with a palpable arrogance.

I had no doubt it was my father. What he was doing there, though, that I couldn't guess. Before I even registered my own actions, I'd pushed away from the table and made it to the door, sliding between Maka and my parents.

Sure enough, my father stood there framed in the doorway, my mother slightly behind him, as usual. I was taken aback by how much like my grandfather my father had come to look in the ten years since I'd seen them. He had that same widow's peak, and his hair was slowly transforming to the snowy white of my grandfather. While he had the same eyes, they lacked the natural warmth and kindness that permeated my grandfather's.

"What the hell are you doing here?" My voice shook, my body itself trembling with anger. "Isn't it bad enough that you came all this way to stalk me, but now you're stalking the people around me, too?"

My father's signature scowl was on his face, and any resemblance to my grandfather I'd seen vanished. "No one is stalking anyone. We're your parents, is it so wrong that we want to reach out to you?"

"Like you've cared these last ten years," I spat bitterly.

Father puffed his chest out, his face purpling. "When that woman you work with told us you'd be here today, we'd hoped you'd be ready to stop acting like a spoiled child and talk to us."

I narrowed my eyes, my stomach dropping. "What lady I work with?"

"Gabe," Grace said hesitantly. I looked and saw she'd gotten up from the table and was standing a foot or so away from me, an uncertain look on her face.

I looked away from her, back to my father, unwilling to accept what my head was telling me. "What lady I work with? The old lady?" It had to be Mrs. Neidermeyer. That was the only answer that was even slightly logical.

"Old lady? No, it was that Asian girl at your office."

"Gabe," Grace said again, voice now desperate instead of hesitant. "I can explain. They came and—"

"What the hell were you thinking, Grace?" I exploded, unable to contain myself. She recoiled back as if I'd struck her, but at that moment, I didn't care. "What gave you the right to do that?"

Grace's words came out quickly. I heard them, but I didn't really process their meaning. "They came to the office today. I had to get something I'd left behind, and they were there, and—"

"I don't care," I interrupted. "There's no excuse. Nothing you could say will make this okay."

"I think we should go," my mother said quietly.

I turned baleful eyes on her. "Yeah, that's a good idea."

They turned and departed, and I rounded back on Grace. She looked like she wanted to say something else, but I had no intentions of giving her the chance. "I trusted you! You *know* how I feel about these people!"

"Gabe," Maka said gently, putting his hands on either of my shoulders. "Maybe you should—"

I shook his hands off. "I can't be here right now."

"Gabe, just listen," Grace pleaded, but I ignored her, storming out of Maka's apartment and slamming the door behind me.

Several hours passed and my anger hadn't abated in the slightest. I sat on my couch, staring at the blank television screen, thinking about just how much Grace had betrayed me.

I'd talked with her countless times about my parents and how I felt about them. This wasn't new information for her. It was something I'd made clear from college when she asked me if I'd be going home for Christmas our freshman year.

That she'd done something like this—telling my parents where they could find me—where my boyfriend would be, that was unacceptable. It wasn't only made worse by the fact that she'd told my parents where my boyfriend lived, information she had no right to disclose.

How could she? It was a question I kept asking myself over and over again. I wasn't interested in an answer, though. I didn't think any answer would be enough.

I wasn't surprised to hear the key rattle in the lock of my door. I'd been expecting Maka would come as soon as he got the rest of the guests gone.

"Hi," he said carefully as he entered. "Have you calmed down any?"

"What do you think?" I huffed.

"I had to check." Maka joined me on the couch, putting one hand on my knee and squeezing comfortingly.

"Aren't you mad?" I demanded.

"You mean because Grace told your parents where I live?" He shrugged. "I admit I'm not exactly thrilled about that, but she didn't really tell complete strangers. I don't think I'm going to have to move over this."

His attempt at humor barely penetrated the haze of anger around me. "I admit I've considered it."

Maka chuckled. "If someone trying to kill you here didn't get you to move, I don't see how something as insignificant as your parents is going to get you to."

I shrugged. "I didn't have the available funds at the time. With the reward from that tontine, I could do it."

"But then we wouldn't be neighbors." Maka moved his hand from my knee, slipping his arm around my shoulders and pulling me against him.

His body radiated heat as always—I called him my personal heat rock—and I found it comforting even in my anger. "You aren't even a little curious about your parents being here in Honolulu?"

I shook my head as best I could with it resting on his shoulder. "Whatever their reason, it can't be good for me."

"And Grace?"

I'd been expecting the question, and it still made me frown. "You think I should forgive her?"

"That's not what I said. Not my call. I'm just asking if you're going to hear her out."

"I don't know," I admitted.

"You'd think she had a reason for it," Maka said, and I couldn't help but think he was right, even though I didn't want to admit it.

"We'll see how I feel tomorrow." Privately, I didn't think that her chances were very high.

Chapter Eight

THE NEXT MORNING my anger hadn't abated. I'd hoped sleep might at least lessen the intensity of it, but it still burned brightly in my chest.

I stopped my phone's alarm and sat on the edge of my bed, shoulders slouched, staring at the patch of floor between my feet. Maybe I would just stay home today. It's not like I had to get anyone's permission to do so, since I was co-owner of the company. It would probably do a world of good for this anger building inside me to avoid seeing Grace. Just thinking about her made it flare up hot in my chest, like heartburn. I had no idea what seeing her would do.

As tempting as it was to avoid her, though, I was needed at work and I knew that. This case was too big for her to work alone. She would need my help, and since I was financially invested in the company, I didn't want to see this case screwed up. Making an enemy of a wealthy woman like Helena Hu struck me as a very bad idea—especially considering we'd already made one wealthy enemy in Manuel Delgado.

As I finished a hastily prepared breakfast of Cheerios and brushed my teeth in the bathroom mirror, I silently reminded myself that I was a professional. Sure, I was pissed as hell at Grace, but that didn't mean I had to allow that to interfere with our professional environment.

We could be pissed at each other and still work together. Ideally, anyway. I was about to find out if that theory worked in practice.

I did my best to calm my anger toward her on the drive to work, listening to Enya in the hopes it would set me in a tranquil mood. At first, I thought it had worked until I arrived at work and saw Grace's Jeep in the parking lot, and the anger bubbled up in me once more, like a cooled tea kettle put back on the fire and brought to a boil once more.

You can still turn around, I told myself. *You haven't turned into the parking lot yet. There's still time.*

I wasn't going to turn around, though, and I knew that. I had to face Grace eventually, so I might as well get it over with now, before the anger could harden into bitterness.

Grace was waiting in the front for me, a cup of Starbucks coffee in hand. When she spoke, her voice had that same tone someone used with a dog they weren't sure was dangerous or not. "Good morning."

I grunted a greeting, not trusting my voice. I was finding it hard enough not to grit my teeth around her.

"I brought coffee." She held the cup toward me, her bearing again reminding me of someone dealing with a dog they were unfamiliar with. The mental analogy itself fueled my anger, even though I knew I couldn't logically blame that on Grace. Logic had gone out the window.

"I had some on the way." My voice sounded frosty even to my own ears, but I didn't care. She had to know that she wouldn't be getting a warm reception from me this morning, and coffee certainly wasn't going to change that. "Give it to Mrs. Neidermeyer when she comes in."

Grace's face fell. "Oh, okay. Listen—"

"What time are Christine's friends coming?" I interrupted, not wanting to give Grace a chance to bring up the previous day.

"Around ten," Grace answered.

"Okay, good. Knock on my door when they get here."

I didn't wait for a reply; I calmly—or more calmly than I would have given myself credit for—made my way to my office and closed my door, maybe more forcefully than I might usually have.

It was no doubt a flight of fantasy of mine, but I imagined Grace standing on the other side of the door, waiting for me to open it, afraid to knock for fear of my reaction. I dismissed that scenario quickly. That wasn't like Grace, no matter how sorry she might be for something.

I tried to tell myself to use the time to focus on work, but my anger didn't allow me to do more than glare at whatever piece of paper I attempted to work with. I was actually grateful when the knock came at my door to signal the arrival of Christine's friends.

Only two of them came—the Caucasian woman and Asian woman from the picture on Christine's fridge. That didn't bother me, considering theirs were the only pictures Christine had displayed so prominently.

They introduced themselves as they came in. The Caucasian woman was Cherie and the Asian woman was Elaina. They both looked nervous to be sitting with us, like they'd never done anything like this at all. I wondered if the police had bothered to seek them out and talk to them, though it was looking like they didn't.

Yet another reason I wondered about the police's involvement. How was it possible they hadn't talked to the friends of the missing woman?

"Thank you for coming in to talk to us," I said, getting the girls situated on the couch in the front office since neither of us had room for four people in our office at the same time.

"Anything, if it means figuring out what happened to Christine," Elaina said, eyes red.

"You guys are going to find her, right?" Cherie asked, reaching over and squeezing Elaina's hand. "The police don't seem to care."

"We're going to try," Grace assured her. "We called you in in hopes that you could answer some questions for us."

"Anything," Elaina repeated.

"Can you tell us about Christine's relationship with Sergio?"

"It was like a fairytale," Cherie said. "It was a whirlwind romance, love at first sight sort of thing."

"I've known Christine since elementary school," Elaina added, "and I'd never seen her happier than when she was with Sergio."

I scribbled a few notes on the notepad I brought. "So Christine was happy with Sergio?"

"She was," Cherie said. "She was in love with Sergio, no doubt."

"So there was no truth to the rumor about Christine and Travis Brent?" Grace asked.

Elaina snorted. "Not a drop. I don't know anyone who knew her who would believe that nonsense. It's just sensationalism in the news. Who doesn't love a scandal involving a rich woman?"

"Travis Brent was her personal assistant," Cherie added. "He was an employee, that's all."

"Where do you think that story came from?" I asked.

Elaina and Cherie shared a look before Elaina finally answered. "I don't know."

"Do you think Sergio suspected them of anything?" I pressed. "Sergio and his father seemed convinced of it."

Cherie rolled her eyes. "I'd be surprised if Sergio noticed anything. He was always busy."

"Do you know anything about a prenup?" Grace asked purposefully, studying the girls for their reactions.

Elaina pursed her lips. "Sergio bring that up, did he?"

"Yes. He told us he and Christine were fighting over it, that she didn't want to sign it."

"Good god," Cherie moaned, rolling her eyes. "Yes, she got a prenup, but it was *her* idea. She's richer than Sergio, and they decided *together* that it was best to protect their assets. Sergio drew it up, Christine had her lawyers look at it, but she was happy with it."

"She had no reason to argue with Sergio about it, then?" I asked, though I knew the answer.

"Not that I can think of," Cherie said, and Elaina nodded her agreement.

The answer didn't surprise me. Everything about Sergio and Manuel Delgado's story seemed suspiciously well-timed to me, a story fabricated to take what were real events—the phone call, the existence of the prenup, the existence of Travis—and weave them into a narrative that they controlled. Conveniently, the only people who could dispute their narrative were missing.

The part that kept me mystified was that the police didn't notice these convenient coincidences that surrounded the Delgados' story.

There wasn't much else to ask them, so we said goodbye to Cherie and Elaina. Once they were gone, I started back toward my office.

"Pretty convenient, huh," Grace said, following behind me.

"What?" I asked, my tone frosty.

"The two completely polar opposite stories from the two camps." Grace sounded surprised that I was talking to her. "You have Sergio who says she hated the prenup and was likely having an affair with her personal assistant, then you have Christine's mother and friends saying that there is no possible way she was having an affair, and she encouraged the prenup."

"And the one story the cops are buying belongs to the man with the money and influence." It wasn't such an unbelievable story, to me.

"That leaves us with still absolutely nothing to go on," Grace said. I walked into my office and she stood hesitantly in the door, like she was uncertain how her passage over the threshold would affect me.

"Until Jin gets back at us with what he finds from the GPS system, anyway," I agreed. It was hard to talk to her, but talking business helped me keep the anger under control, gave me something to focus on.

"There's still a chance that nothing will come of this," Grace said, crossing the doorway and entering my office. She still lingered by the door, though, keeping her distance.

"There's always that chance," I said flatly, pulling a file—any file, it didn't matter—out and flopping it open in front of me. Looking at anything but Grace was a good idea.

"Gabe," Grace started. I heard that tone in her voice, knew what path she was about to start us down, and held up my hand to cut her off.

"No, Grace. I don't want to talk about it."

"I just wanted to—"

"We're at work, Grace, so I'd like to *not* discuss personal matters."

Grace let out a snort. "Since when?"

I gritted my teeth to swallow back an angry outburst. "Since today." I couldn't see her face, but I hoped her silence indicated she could read the cues in my voice and wasn't about to push me further.

"Gabe, it might not be my place, but—"

And there it was: she pushed me much further than I was willing to go.

"*Might not* be your place?" I repeated, nearly giving myself whiplash looking up at her. "*Might not*? Grace, there's no *might* in that sentence. You had no right to talk to my parents about me, even if they did come here while you were here. You had no right to give them Maka's information, or tell them where I'd be. I don't know what you were hoping to accomplish by orchestrating that little meet-up, but all you did was royally piss me off."

Grace flinched a little bit but didn't back down. "I know that. You've made that pretty clear. But I did have a reason for doing that."

"Oh, you did? I'm glad that you had a reason for doing it, since you know exactly how I feel about my parents! Do tell, Grace. Tell me exactly what reason there was for you to go sticking your nose where it didn't belong and completely shatter my trust."

I didn't realize I was on my feet or that I was shouting until I stopped and my office echoed in the silence that followed. My face felt hot, my temples pulsed as blood rushed through me. I was propping my hands on my desk, and my arms trembled.

The look on Grace's face caught me off-guard. She'd paled, her eyes were wide, like she was seeing me for the first time.

She closed the door, though it was a little late for that.

When she spoke, though, her voice was even. "I'm going to take that as an invitation to actually talk to you—or was the question rhetorical?"

I didn't say anything—I couldn't find my voice at the moment anyway—so she went on.

"Yes, we've talked about your parents. I understand your relationship with them as much as I can. You know what I've never wanted to do? Talk about my relationship with *my* parents."

I had never thought about it before, but now that I did, I realized she was right. I couldn't recall ever hearing about her family, beyond mentions of her aunt.

Grace started to pace in a little circle in front of my desk, rubbing her hands together. "My father was a Methodist preacher, my mother the model preacher's wife. I guess that's just a fancy way of saying that she was a weak-willed flower, conceding to his every whim, at least in her case. I had no freedom—strict curfew, they never let me go out with friends, or attend parties or sleepovers. I had to be this perfect girl."

I slowly sat down as her story unfolded. "I know a little bit about needing to fit a certain image."

"One day, my sophomore year of high school, a friend convinced me to go with her instead of going home. She was basically one of the few friends I was able to keep, considering the rules my father had. I don't know what made me say yes, but finally I did.

"We went to her house, first, and played around like normal teenage girls. I couldn't help but worry the whole time that my father would be furious, but I had fun."

She chuckled at something, then, whether at her worries or something she was remembering from the day I didn't know.

"Eventually she got a message from a couple of her friends, people I didn't know, and we agreed to go meet with them. By that point, I wanted to go home, but I didn't want to look uncool. There was a thrill to it all, too. I was excited to be free. They brought alcohol—Zimas, actually—and we drank them in a park. I only had a few sips, that's all, I wasn't brave enough to do more. I was basically a teenage version of my mother."

I was trying to imagine Grace like that, and I was having a hard time doing so. The Grace I'd always known was fierce and independent and confident. She did what she wanted and there wasn't anyone out there who could control her. It was the sort of mentality that led to her working somewhere like Paradise Investigations, where she didn't really answer to anyone but the client, and most clients let us do what we thought best, trusting in the expertise of those they hired.

"That didn't matter to the police, though. They caught us. My father had to be called to come pick me up from the station. He was so angry. He thought I was acting out on purpose, that I was trying to make him look bad. He ranted at me for hours that night. My mom just sat there and listened."

She finally sat down, like her body was deflating. Telling the story was difficult, I supposed. "From that point on things were different between us. I resented their control, their chains. I started acting out on purpose. Junior year I met a boy I really liked. Ironically, he went to my church. Well, we were teenagers. One day we decided that instead of our usual Wednesday night youth group meeting we found an empty room and just kissed. Nothing more than that—nothing dirty at all, just kissing. My father caught us."

Grace went quiet for a moment. "He didn't rant that time, didn't scold or lecture me. Didn't say anything. The next morning my mother told me to pack my belongings. They were sending me to live with my aunt—his sister."

The emotion had finally seeped into her voice, and for a moment I thought she might burst into tears. "For three months I tried to call home, every day. No one answered. No one returned any messages I left. My aunt didn't want to take me to see them. Finally I went on my own. Took a taxi. My mother opened the door—I knew my father wouldn't be home, but if I could talk to my mother that would have made me feel *somewhat* better."

"And what happened?" I asked. My anger hadn't abated, but it had cooled a bit, at least.

"She told me that I was a selfish child. She told me that I'd embarrassed them enough. Since I clearly had no respect for them, I was no longer welcome in their home."

I had been expecting the answer—it's the only one that would make sense of why she was telling me this story in the first place—but it was still disheartening to hear. Why was it so hard for parents to accept and love their children?

"I kept trying. I sent them invitations to my high school graduation. They didn't come. Then, I reached out to them several times in college. They had no interest. I found out our senior year that my father died. Heart disease."

I furrowed my brow. "Senior year? Why didn't you ever say...oh." I thought about it, the connection made in my head. "That's when you disappeared for five or six days in the fall, right?"

Grace nodded. "I went to the funeral, and then needed some time for myself. Even after my father's death, though, my mother still has no desire to reach out to me. None whatsoever, no matter how many times I tried."

She reached across the desk and took my hand, and I let her. She looked into my eyes, her own shiny with unspilt tears. "My parents had no desire to repair our relationship, I doubt the thought ever passed their minds. My mother didn't tell me about my father's death, my aunt did. She didn't acknowledge my presence."

She cleared her throat, releasing my hands. "I know your parents treated you awfully, and I know you're mad at them for good reason. But my parents, they never even attempted to make amends. Maybe yours want to. I just wish you'd think about that before you write them off entirely."

Grace got up then and left quickly, no doubt wanting to get out before I had the chance to send a comeback her way. The truth was, I didn't have a comeback for her. I was still angry, and I still wholeheartedly believed she'd done the wrong thing, but it was somewhat comforting to see she'd had a reason for doing it. She thought she was helping, and even I thought that had to count for something.

But what did she want me to do about it? Was I supposed to forgive eighteen years of bad parenting and ten years of silence? We'd gotten along just fine pretending that the other never existed, why should I change that now? And why did she think the onus belonged on me?

Then again, my parents had traveled a long way to come and see me, not to mention submitted themselves to multiple rejections. That was uncharacteristic of my parents. Even they wouldn't have been arrogant enough to just assume I would welcome their appearance with open arms.

Could it be possible that my parents were actually here to make amends? And even if it was, was I ready to forgive?

I spent the most of the remainder of the work day lost in thought about that. I couldn't argue that people didn't change, because I knew they could. I had, even in the small time I'd been in Hawai'i.

I was startled from the constant waffling train of thought by Grace knocking on my door. "I'm heading home. There's not much else we can do on the case until we hear back from Jin or get another lead."

"Okay," I answered curtly. Grace sighed and started out. I don't know what exactly made me feel bad for her, but something about her downcast expression tugged at my heartstrings and made me call out to her. "Hey, wait up. I'll head out, too. No use in me hanging around here."

"You know," Grace commented as she locked the front door behind us, "I'm glad that Mrs. Neidermeyer is always off on Mondays."

I laughed a little bit, despite myself. "Yeah, she would have had a field day over that yelling match."

"You did all the yelling," Grace reminded me, though her voice was less accusatory than it might have been; she was still walking on eggshells around me, a bit, and I appreciated it. I was still angry—and with good reason, I thought—and wasn't quite ready to let go of it.

On the way to my car, I stopped suddenly. The hair on the back of my neck was standing up, and the feeling of being watched hit me again. I looked around, trying to find the source. My eyes passed over them twice before finally settling on them a third time. There—across the street from Paradise Investigations—two men walked casually, like they were out and about doing their own thing. I would have thought they were, except they turned to face me, and I saw that they were the same men who were outside my condo.

There was no way it was a coincidence they were there in front of my office after also being spotted in front of my condo. The same guy who made eye contact with me in front of the condo made contact with me again. He didn't look away, didn't do the normal "cursory eye contact, look away" thing strangers did. No, he held my eyes as he walked until it would have been too awkward to keep eye contact.

A cold lump formed in my stomach and remained there as I watched them walk away.

"Uh, Gabe, are you okay?" Grace asked, putting her hand on my shoulder. "What are you looking at?"

"Nothing," I told her absently. The men had vanished from sight, but something told me they weren't far away. "Nothing at all."

Chapter Nine

I SLEPT BADLY that night, my dreams filled with the sensation of being watched or chased. Every time I woke from the dream, I would slip right back into something similar. I wished Maka had been there; I would have slept easier with him beside me, but he had a long night at work so I was on my own.

The sensation of the dreams followed me Tuesday morning as I showered and drank down a cup of coffee before going in to work. I couldn't manage to shake the feeling, no matter how hard I tried.

The one good thing about it was that it distracted me from my anger at Grace, so by the time I arrived at Paradise Investigations, I was only slightly irritated with her.

Since it was Tuesday, Mrs. Neidermeyer was back at work, but she was reasonably dressed in a leopard print sweat suit ensemble that said "Bootylicious" in sequins on the butt. It was a definite step up from some of her previous outfits, so I decided not to make too much of a big deal out of it.

"You look tired this morning," Mrs. Neidermeyer remarked, giving me the once over. "Maka keep you up all night?"

I was really glad I didn't have a drink, because if I did it would have gone flying. "Mrs. Neidermeyer!"

"What? If I had a guy as sexy as Maka, I'd be constantly tired, too."

I didn't want to, but my brain rebelled and began to conjure images of Mrs. Neidermeyer with *anyone*, and my already bad start to the day just got worse.

"There needs to be a rule in the workplace about discussing things like that," I told her. "Consider it set in place as of now."

She exhaled loudly through her nose. "I see Grace's prudishness is rubbing off on you."

"I'm not a prude and neither is she," I chided. "There are just some conversation topics that aren't appropriate for the workplace."

Behind me the front door opened, the bell attached to it jingling.

"Is he here?" Grace asked quickly, the words running together to sound more like 'izeear?' Her purse was hanging on the crook of her arm, having clearly slid down from her shoulder. I guessed she'd run in from her car.

"Is who here?" I asked, having no idea what she was talking about.

"Jin," she said, and I realized how obvious it had been. Before nine in the morning I was terrible at my job. "He messaged me to say he was getting ready to head over here. He hasn't come in yet?"

"Did you see his car in the parking lot?"

Grace frowned. "Oh. Right. I'm useless without coffee." I didn't comment on it, but it was remarkable how similar our thought processes were. Grace stalked to the coffee pot and poured herself a cup, taking a slow sip before she let out a satisfied sigh. "Hopefully Jin is coming to tell us something good."

"Maybe he's coming to ask you on a date," I added, mostly to see her squirm.

"Don't even. After the travesty the last few times we've met up? I wouldn't be surprised if he told us this was the last case he wants to consult with us on."

We didn't have long to wait, thankfully. Grace hadn't even gotten halfway through the cup of coffee when Jin came through the door, his laptop tucked under his arm.

"Morning, everyone."

"Jin, you look more dashing every time I see you," Mrs. Neidermeyer said, voice becoming something like a purr. "If I was ten years younger—"

"Only ten years?" Grace muttered, scowling. She poured a cup of coffee for Jin, who took it gratefully. As she walked by Mrs. Neidermeyer's desk, I distinctly heard her whisper "Keep it in your pants, old lady."

Mrs. Neidermeyer drew herself up haughtily, and didn't bother to lower her voice. "Threatened by an 'old lady,' Grace?"

"Okay," I said, heading off a fight and a moment that would probably have been awkward for both Jin and myself. "Jin, you have something for us?"

"Yeah. I've got all the relevant data from Christine Hu's GPS system."

"Well, let's get to work then, okay?" I held the door to the offices open for Jin to go through, waving Grace to go on ahead of me. Once they were both through, I pointed my finger warningly at Mrs. Neidermeyer, who just gave me this wide-eyed, innocent look I didn't buy for a moment.

"You know, Jin," Grace was saying when I walked into her office where Jin was setting up his laptop, "we should just turn the third room into an office for you here, as much work as you do for us."

I could guess how she meant it to sound, but it came across like every romantic comedy where there's the one person who just fails miserably at flirting every time they try. Even the little laugh she followed it with sounded forced and desperate.

It was hard for me to hold on to what remained of my anger toward her when she kept punishing herself so harshly. It was like Jin was her romantic kryptonite. Every time he was around, she turned into this sort of more awkward version of herself.

As her friend, it fell to me to help her out in times like those, so I cleared my throat before that one could really settle and brought everyone's attention back to why we were actually there.

"All right, Jin, what do you have for us?"

Jin hit a few buttons on the computer and the screen popped to life. The web browser was open to a page that listed several geographic coordinates.

"These are the locations her GPS recorded her car being at. For it to have registered she needed to be in one spot long enough for it to ping the company's server that location, which happens periodically to provide better navigating services."

"So far I'm understanding all of this," Grace said, sounding pleased with herself.

Jin smiled. "It's not all that complicated. I used the phone call timing that you gave me and isolated the places that her car was after that. There were just four. This one, here—" Jin double clicked on one of them and a map popped out. "—is her address, based on the information you gave me. She was there most of the day after the phone call, until about six that evening."

"Where did she go after that?" I asked, though I had a few suspicions.

Jin clicked on the second. "Around six o'clock, she was picked up by the GPS service here."

I recognized the address immediately. "That's Delgado's office building."

Jin nodded. "Right. She was there until eight o'clock or so. Then she was on the move again. The next place her car remained for any length of time was here."

A third click and location popped up. It didn't make any sense to me at first, but then it became clear. It was one of the island's many dockside areas. From the looks of it, it was privately owned, probably by a shipping company.

"Is that a warehouse?" Grace asked, moving closer to the screen for a better look.

"It is. Her car was there for several hours. It finally turned up here." He clicked to the final location, which was easily recognizable as the Honolulu airport. "At two in the morning."

I blinked. "At *two*? Who would be showing up at the airport for a flight at two? No one shows up *that* early."

"Just what I was thinking. I also can't think of a reason she'd go to this warehouse location," Jin added. "I pulled it up on Google, and it belongs to a shipping company called Dostavka. As far as I know there's no connection at all between Christine Hu and that company."

"Well, she's got a lot of wealthy connections. Maybe she knows the owner," I suggested. "We won't know that until we talk to Helena Hu about it. But none of this looks very good for Christine."

"I think we're forgetting something pretty important here," Grace said. "We have no proof that it was Christine who drove to any of these places, only that her car went there. Someone else could have been behind the wheel."

She was right, I hadn't thought of that, and I didn't really like the implications of it. "You mean someone wants everyone to think that she took a flight so drove her car to the airport where it would eventually be identified?" Grace nodded solemnly, even though it was a rhetorical question. "Do you think that it was the personal assistant, Travis?"

"We know next to nothing about this guy, so I honestly don't have any idea."

"If she didn't drive the car, then where is Christine?" Jin asked. Neither Grace nor I could answer that question for certain, though I did have an idea I didn't like.

"Well...the warehouse is on the ocean, right?"

Grace saw the direction I was taking that and decided to head it off. "Let's not jump to conclusions, okay? We should stick to the facts until we know more."

The bell over the front door chimed loudly, bringing our musings to a halt. As far as I know we weren't expecting anyone, and the surprise on Grace's face told me I was right.

Panic clawed its way up my chest as I thought about the two men I'd seen across the street and in front of my condo. I was beginning to regret not telling Maka about them. Mrs. Neidermeyer hadn't called out for help, though, so I took that as a good sign.

Then again, she could be dead, which would probably make Grace happy.

I led the way into the front and much to my surprise found Braeden Jeffords standing there, a messenger bag slung over his shoulder. I resisted the urge to swear mostly because it was still work hours, but I barely held it in.

"What are you doing here, Mr. Jeffords? I made it clear that I didn't want you following me. Are you being willfully difficult or are you trying to call my bluff?"

Jeffords held his hands up defensively. "Hey, don't go calling that police officer boyfriend of yours. I have an appointment."

I rounded on Mrs. Neidermeyer. I hadn't heard the phone ring.

Mrs. Neidermeyer chuckled and looked at the calendar on her desk. "Oh yeah. He called and made the appointment on Saturday."

"And you forgot to tell us?" I said through gritted teeth.

"You sound surprised," Grace muttered.

"It may have slipped my mind," Mrs. Neidermeyer admitted, sounding utterly unrepentant. I was adding that to the list of things I needed to talk to her about in the near future.

"I'll get going, then," Jin said after an awkward pause.

"Thanks for the help, Jin," I said, shaking his hand.

"You know where to send the invoice," Grace added with a too-wide smile. When Jin turned his back, she shot me a *Help me!* look. Whatever slump she'd found herself in, it was hitting her hard. I hoped she would shake it off soon.

Once Jin was gone Braeden Jeffords said, "So we going to sit down and talk?"

"We're not looking for a member of the paparazzi right now," I said, turning my back to him. To Mrs. Neidermeyer I said, "I'm going back to my office."

"I can help you," Jeffords called, but I ignored him. "I can say with certainty that Christine Hu and Travis Brent weren't romantically involved."

That caught my attention. Grace and I shared a look before turning back to him. He patted his messenger bag to indicate that he had the proof we sought inside. I was hesitant to trust him, but decided to leave this to Grace.

"We'll give you five minutes," Grace said shortly. "And we're charging you for the full consultation."

I didn't like the idea of working with Braeden Jeffords, but at that point, I was willing to take whatever help we could get on this one. I didn't expect him to be all that helpful, but I was willing to try anything.

"I've spent a long time following Christine Hu," Jeffords began as he followed behind us. Grace took the lead and led us into *my* office. I grumbled about that under my breath, but there wasn't much I could do about it now.

"That's not creepy at all," Grace said dryly, stepping behind my desk and making room for me to slip past her and into my chair. "Why would you be following her, anyway? She doesn't seem the type to catch the interest of the paparazzi."

"Maybe not now, but there was a time when she was."

"Oh, really?" I asked before I could control the impulse.

"Definitely. She was a wild child in her late teens. I don't know what made her calm down, but she did. I've been following her off and on since then, hoping for some sign of her old ways to come out."

"And you wonder why people think that paparazzi are garbage." Grace glowered at Jeffords, who shrugged unapologetically.

"It's a job that needs doing. Face it: people like seeing celebrities and rich people failing. It helps them feel better about their own lives."

I waved my hand impatiently. "You said something about proof Christine and her personal assistant weren't sleeping together?"

Jeffords nodded, unpacking his laptop and turning it on. "I've got thousands of pictures of Christine on my computer—" Grace made a noise of disgust that Jeffords ignored. "—dating back to around the date of the announcement of her engagement to Sergio Delgado. I figured if I doubled down, I might be able to uncover a marriage scandal between them. Imagine the money I'd make from that!"

"What you're saying is you were purposefully *looking* for any indication that one of them was cheating," I clarified, and Jeffords nodded. "Okay, so you found no proof?"

Jeffords opened a file on the computer and a huge collection of photos popped up. He clicked on one and enlarged it. It was a picture of Christine Hu coming out of a restaurant. "This was about a week ago. She went out to lunch."

"Okay," Grace said, clearly missing the point that Jeffords was making. I didn't quite see it, either, if I was being honest.

"Look here. She was at the restaurant for two hours—I was there the whole time." He clicked on a picture before it. "This is when she went in. Here's Travis Brent. He waited outside the whole time."

I sighed to myself. A picture them *not* having lunch together one time was not strong evidence, as I expected.

He pulled up several more pictures at the same time and clicked through them slowly. "I started taking these off and on before the wedding announcement was made, and started doing it regularly after. In *every single one* Travis Brent waits outside or goes somewhere else for lunch."

"So Delgado or supporters of his theory would just say they were being very careful in public," Grace said, playing devil's advocate.

"True. But I've also never seen any indication of Travis Brent entering her apartment. He's never even been there as far as I can tell."

"Hotels," I reasoned.

"I thought that too. I spent every night for a week alternating either being at Christine's apartment building or Travis Brent's place. They never crossed paths outside of their professional relationship. Then there's this."

He showed us several photos of Travis Brent out to romantic dinners or on dates with a woman I recognized as Jennifer from Halimer and Gold.

"That's Jennifer. She works at the same agency that Travis Brent does—or did. She said they were together."

"And this is proof that they were," Jeffords said.

"Still doesn't prove that Christine and he weren't," Grace said patiently. "Plenty of people have two lovers. It's not outside the realm of possibility."

"Can we skim through some of the more recent pictures?" I asked. I didn't expect to find anything, but I felt like I might as well give these thorough attention since he was there.

Jeffords opened another file. "These are all from a week before she disappeared leading to the day before."

"Why didn't you follow her on the day she disappeared?" Grace asked. "That would have been the most useful."

Jeffords looked sheepish. "Hey, I had to go to the hospital. My baby niece was born that day."

I clicked through the pictures, not paying much attention to either of them. I didn't really know what I was looking for in them, but there had to be something there—maybe something in her face that showed she was unhappy enough to just hop on a plane, or a sign that she was scared of *something*, but I didn't see it. She just looked like a happy, busy woman.

On the first look I missed it, but something made me go back to the picture I was just looking at—a picture of Christine in an art gallery—and study it closer. Barely in the frame but enough that I could see his face clearly was the same man I'd seen outside my condo.

I quickly rechecked other pictures, and out of fifteen I saw the man and/or his partner in eleven. That was *not* a coincidence.

"Who are these men?" I asked Jeffords.

He leaned over to look at what I meant and shrugged. "No idea. Just some guys."

"You're sure?" I went to another picture with them and pointed them out, and then did it again.

"I never noticed them like that," Jeffords admitted.

"Wait...weren't those guys across the street?" Grace asked, a slightly accusatory tone in her voice. "The ones you were looking at yesterday?" I nodded and she slapped my arm. "The same ones that were outside your condo?" I nodded again and she slapped me again. "Why didn't you tell me?"

"Because I couldn't be sure it was more than just a bad feeling about them or a weird coincidence," I said defensively, rubbing my arm where she hit me.

"Well, are you sure now?"

"Very. As sure as I am that these men are involved with Delgado somehow." I stood up, reaching a hand out to Jeffords to shake his hand.

"I'm really surprised that I'm saying this, Mr. Jeffords, but thank you. You've been a huge help. How much can we pay you for the pictures?"

"I don't want money." Something in the way he said that made me hesitate. Paparazzi were notoriously slimy, and something told me that he was about to use the pictures for some pretty big leverage.

"Okay…what do you want?"

"I want exclusive rights to write this story. I want to be the only person you give an interview to—and Helena Hu, as well."

"You're a photographer, not a journalist."

Jeffords flashed a shark-like smile, all teeth. "Some of us have greater ambitions, Mr. Maxfield. Besides, I can sell the interview to whatever outlet I want and make more money than you two would be willing to pay me, even with your treasure hunter money."

It was a no-brainer. Sure, I thought it was disgusting that he was going to try to advance his career on the potential misfortune of a human being, but *someone* would write about it, and his pictures had proven more helpful than I possibly could have anticipated.

"You have a deal."

GRACE AND I followed Jeffords out the door after printing off a large slew of the pictures and were off to see if the photographs would encourage Delgado to be more forthcoming. It probably wouldn't, but it might put him on notice that we recognized his goons and he might call them off, or else get nervous and make a mistake.

It was nearly one in the afternoon, so we figured that lunch break would be just about over for the company, so it was as good a time as any.

"How do you want to handle this?" Grace asked in a low voice as we made our way across the parking lot.

"Well, we just go and show him the pictures and let him know we're on to him. Hopefully it shakes him up enough to make him reveal something, even if it's just with his face. That's the only way we're ever going to get an advantage over him."

"It's probably not going to make him talk, you know."

I did know that, and that wasn't my goal. A man like Manuel Delgado wasn't going to be intimidated by the pair of us. But he could be put on notice, and that was my goal.

The woman at the desk turned hard eyes on us as we entered, and I got the feeling we weren't welcome. I couldn't imagine her giving that frosty greeting to everyone who came in.

"Can I help you?"

"We'd like to speak with Mr. Delgado, please," I said, voice as warm and inviting as I could make it.

"Do you have an appointment?" she asked in a tone that made it clear that she knew that we didn't.

"No, but we won't take up much of his time."

"I'm sorry, he's extremely busy. No appointment, no entry."

"I'm sure if you just call him—"

"No appointment, no entry," she repeated firmly.

"Well then," Grace said sweetly, "when is his next available appointment?"

The secretary looked between us, unblinking. "May."

"You've got to be kidding me," Grace exploded, but I just put a hand calmingly on her elbow.

"Thank you for your time. I guess we'll be going now."

The woman grunted and turned back to her work.

"You're just going to give up?" Grace hissed as we exited the building.

"No, of course not. There's no use trying to push it here, though. It's going to be impossible to get to him at work."

"I doubt he'll see us at his home, either. So what are we going to do?" I raised my eyebrows at her, and she frowned. "I don't like that look. What are you thinking?"

"I'm thinking that we're going to have to get a little creative."

Chapter Ten

THE BEGINNING OF a plan had formed in my head by the time we returned to Paradise Investigations. I had Mrs. Neidermeyer put a call in to Helena Hu, asking her to meet us there at the office. She was there barely twenty minutes later.

Grace and I walked her through what we'd discovered so far, and I showed her the pictures of the men I'd seen. "Have you noticed these men around?" I asked as she studied the photos closely.

"Not that I can remember, but that doesn't mean I haven't. I see a lot of people every day; I've learned to just tune out most of their faces. I'll show them to my security team, see if they come up with anything." She looked up from the picture, then, catching and holding my gaze. "Do you think these men have anything to do with Manuel Delgado?"

"We don't know for sure," I said cautiously. "But we do think there could be a connection. We want to bring this up to Delgado, but he's keeping us out with security."

"Convenient."

And now we'd come to the bit of a long shot plan I'd started on. "Right. But, I had an idea. We can't approach Delgado at work, and I'm sure we can't get to him at home, but if we get to him between those destinations, we might have an easier time getting him to talk."

Helena thought for a moment, tapping her finger against her chin. "I may have something for that. Give me twenty minutes." She didn't wait for our response—she didn't need to; she was the boss, it wasn't like we could have said no—but pulled her phone from her pocket and stepped outside.

"I like her a lot," Mrs. Neidermeyer said from the doorway that led to the front of the building. "That's a woman with style and power." She shot a look Grace's way. "Nice to have one of them around."

Grace jabbed a finger in her direction. "You're already on thin ice. You do know that a secretary's job is to tell her employer when there's been an appointment made, right?"

"Oh? Is that right?" Mrs. Neidermeyer feigned lack of understanding. "From what I hear some employers actually *ask* their secretaries if there have been any appointments made."

"We shouldn't have to—"

"Okay, okay," I interrupted, not wanting to listen to the two of them bicker. "No fighting in front of the clients. You both agreed to that rule." Both of them looked like they were going to say something in retort but I made a sharp *zip it* gesture across my mouth and they both remained quiet.

Helena returned after only ten minutes, a victorious look on her face. "That was easier than I thought it would be. Manuel Delgado likes to schmooze about, show up at the well-known restaurants, hot spots in town. I had my people call around and find out where he has a reservation tonight."

Grace made a sound deep in her throat. "I wish I could pull that kind of sway."

"You'd use it for evil," I said dryly. "So, Mrs. Hu, where is he going to be tonight?"

"Have you ever heard of Longitude?"

If I'd been a cartoon character my jaw would have dropped to the floor. Had I heard of Longitude? Of course I had! Everybody knew about the place. It had only been open for two months, a new place near Waikiki owned by one of those famous celebrity chefs with the cooking competitions on television. It was also, according to Maka who had a surprising passion about all things cooking-show related, pretty much guaranteed a Michelin star in the near future.

"I would literally kill to get into that place!" Grace exclaimed, close enough to me that I winced at the sound.

"That's the only way you'd get into one," Mrs. Neidermeyer said under her breath but loud enough for me to hear. I hid my smile from Grace and gave Mrs. Neidermeyer a warning look.

"Well, I'll spare you the second murder charge," Helena said, and for a moment I couldn't believe that she'd just made a joke. It was completely out of character and yet perfectly poised, without missing a beat or batting an eye. "I've got you on the list. Your reservation is for eight-fifteen, fifteen minutes after Delgado's. After that, it's up to you. Oh, and by the way, wear something nice."

Helena took her leave, then. Grace waited until she was gone before clapping her hands excitedly. "Undercover work! Score!"

"We're not going undercover, Grace. Delgado knows who we are."

"Hey, I get to dress up and then charge the dry-cleaning fee to Helena. Let me have this."

GRACE INSISTED ON driving, saying that my reliance on the car's GPS made her uncomfortable. At just after seven I was dressed in the nicest suit I owned, pictures we needed to confront Delgado with tucked under my arm. I stood in front of the mirror in my bedroom, adjusting my tie.

"Damn, you look good," Maka said from where he leaned against the bedroom doorway. In the mirror I could see his eyes traveling my form appreciatively. I didn't bother hiding how pleased his attention made me. Everybody wanted to be appreciated, right?

Tie finished, I turned around to face him. "You think so?"

"Definitely." Maka straightened, walking toward me, heat in his eyes. "Why is it you get more dressed up for a night out with Grace than you do for a night out with me?"

I slid my arms around Maka's solid frame, fingers lacing together against his back. "Well, maybe if you took me to a place like Longitude once and a while, I'd get dressed up for you, too."

Maka tried to pull away from me, scowling, but I held on tightly, laughing. "I'm kidding. You know I'll wear whatever you ask me to wear." Maka's eyebrows rose up at that and I regretted the words, feeling the need to quickly add, "Within reason."

"I'm going to pretend I didn't hear that last part," Maka said, like I knew he would. He captured my lips in a quick kiss. "Oh, the things I could ask you to wear."

I could feel his excitement at the prospect pressed against me, and my body began to respond in kind, so I reluctantly stepped away from him before my body got too far out of my control.

"You just keep thinking about those until I get home, and we'll see what we can do. Grace will unfortunately show up at any moment."

As if she was waiting for her cue, I heard her Jeep pull into the parking lot in front of my condo. A moment later, the blast of her horn made me wince. Why didn't she just call or text to say she was here like everybody else?

"Well, wish me luck."

"Just don't get arrested," Maka said, face and voice serious.

I rolled my eyes. "You're so supportive."

"Or murdered," Maka added, following me to the front door. "Or kidnapped."

"That only happened once, and it was mostly your idea," I reminded him, giving him one last kiss goodbye.

I climbed into the Jeep and Maka waved at me until I rolled the window down. "Make sure you bring me a doggy bag, okay? I want to try this place, too!"

Once Maka returned inside I looked to Grace, who hadn't made any effort to leave the parking lot. "What are you waiting for?"

"I'm waiting for a 'Hey, Grace, you look nice,' since that would be polite."

I crossed my arms over my chest. "I didn't hear you offering up any compliments when I got in." Grace harrumphed and I chuckled. "You look great, Grace."

She did, too. She wore a beautiful purple take on the little black dress that wouldn't be out of place in a nice restaurant like Longitude or on the floor of a dance club. "This is the dress that you should wear when you hang out with Jin."

Beaming happily, Grace put the car in reverse. The radio blasted as we started toward Waikiki and Longitude, but I had little patience for the new Taylor Swift song that seemed to be playing nonstop on the radio, so I quickly flicked it off.

I actually ended up regretting that when Grace decided to fill the silence with conversation, instead. "Have you thought about what I said about your parents?"

I sighed louder than a rebellious teenager. "Are you *sure* this is a topic you want to bring up, Grace? You're not entirely out of the woods on this one."

"Come on, Gabe, you know I'm right."

"Those don't sound like words I would actually think," I said crossly. Why did she have to keep bringing this up? I understood—now—her own emotional investment in it, but why couldn't she understand my situation was different than hers? She'd been rejected, where I'd done the rejecting. I could understand that she had a need for closure, but I didn't.

"How would you feel if something bad happened to your parents and you never got to talk to them?"

I shrugged. "I don't have anything else to say to them."

"It seems like they've got something they want to say to you. Don't glare at me like that," she added. "I'm trying to help you, even if you're too stubborn to see that."

"What it sounds like to me is that you're trying to get involved in something that has nothing to do with you. Please don't."

Grace wasn't one to be cowed, though, and I knew that, so I wasn't at all surprised when she took only a few seconds to continue her campaign. "What would you do if your parents' plane crashed on their way back home? How would you feel, knowing you rejected them? Would you honestly be okay with that?"

I banged my head against the glass of the passenger side door window. "Fine, fine, fine! If it will make you *stop* I'll meet with them for five freaking minutes. Are you happy?"

"I'll be happier when you realize what a great idea this is and thank me afterward."

I opened my mouth to say something clever—I hadn't exactly thought of it yet, but I was hoping it was clever—but Grace preemptively cut me off. "Oh look, we're here!"

Longitude was extremely upscale. It reminded me of the sort of place my parents would go to in order to be seen. The building was all sleek and modern, lots of glass, though it was tinted to shield the diners within from view. The place even had valet parking, which put it in another tier entirely from the places that I'd grown accustomed to eating since leaving for college.

I was self-conscious getting out of Grace's Jeep right in front of the restaurant in order to pass it to the valet. The other cars there were no doubt in a completely different price bracket, and the Wrangler brought attention our way. It wasn't the most undercover of entrances we could have accomplished, but thanks to the tint, I doubted Delgado could see us, even if his table was right next to a window.

Grace seemed completely unbothered by our mode of transportation, handing the keys to the valet just like they were the keys to a Ferrari.

As the valet drove off with the Jeep, she slipped her arm through mine, resting her hand on the crook of my elbow. "Ready?"

I smiled and nodded and we entered Longitude.

The moment we stepped through the door, we were met with a wave of sensory input. The air was heavy with the competing aroma of various dishes—hints of spice, the smell of meat, the heady bouquet of fine wines—and the sound of glasses clinking and cutlery striking against plates, and beneath that the constant hum of conversation. The lighting was low and calming, and there was enough space between the tables to ensure conversations could happen in relative privacy.

"This place is gorgeous," I murmured to Grace as we approached the maître d's stand. The man standing attentively at the post wore a suit that no doubt cost much more than my own. He was balding, his face set with a weak chin and a thin mouth that turned down into the slightest hint of a frown when we stood in front of his podium.

"May I help you?"

"We have reservations," Grace said demurely, giving him her friendliest smile. "Under Park and Maxfield, I believe."

The maître d' checked his list, running a bony finger down it until he came to our names and tapped it gently. "Ah, yes, right here. Your table is ready, so if you would follow me."

He led us through the space between the tables, and I kept a sharp eye out for Delgado while trying to not look like I was scanning the room for people. Most of the diners paid us no attention; wealthy citizens and socialites with no time for someone of a lower status or someone who couldn't somehow benefit their image or position in society.

Right before we arrived at our table, I spotted Delgado. He was at a table toward the center of the room but not near our own. He was seated alone at the moment, a glass of white wine in hand as he perused the menu. Every now and then someone would walk by and he would exchange a few words with them, pleasant smile plastered on his face. The man was good at putting on a show.

Well, soon he'd see that so were we.

"Delgado's right over there," I told Grace once the maître d' had retreated, pointing discreetly toward his table.

"He doesn't have his food yet," Grace said, picking up the menu. "Means we have time to order."

I couldn't believe her. "We're not here for dinner!"

"Come on, when else are we going to get a chance to try this place? And it would be on Helena's dime!" I maintained my incredulous stare until she sighed in defeat. "Okay, okay, you're right. Work is the priority."

We rose from our seats together, me with the photos in their manila folder tucked carefully under my arm. A few nearby diners glanced up at us, and I gave them friendly passing smiles and they turned their attention back to their dinners.

Maybe Manny Delgado sensed our presence, because he looked up just as we reached his table. He looked less than pleased by our arrival.

"Mr. Delgado, how good to see you here," I said loudly enough to draw the attention of the neighboring tables, a subtle hint to him that I was more than willing to cause a scene.

"Mr. Maxfield, Ms. Park," Delgado greeted coolly. "I wish I could say the same. The two of you are certainly persistent."

"It's part of what makes us good at our jobs," Grace said, choosing to take it for a compliment when it obviously wasn't. "It was just a stroke of good fortune we found you here tonight."

"I'm sure." Delgado's glower lacked some of its power in the restaurant surrounded by people. "Well, you two should get back to your table. I'm sure you wouldn't want to delay your dinner. The beef Wellington is sublime. I recommend it."

"Before we do that, there's something I'd like to show you, Mr. Delgado." I pulled the photographs out and placed them on the table directly in front of him, ignoring his frustrated noises. "Would you happen to recognize either of these men in the photos, Mr. Delgado?"

He barely ran his eyes over them, but there was a subtle shifting in his bearing, I thought, though I might have been imagining it. "No."

"Are you sure? Because these men keep turning up in a lot of places your future daughter-in-law was recently. And after our conversation with you and your son, they started turning up wherever we are, as well. Pretty convenient, right?"

"Depends on your definition of convenient," Delgado answered mildly, taking a slow sip from his wine glass. "Why don't you come right out and say it, hm? That's what you've come here to do, right? Find me in a public place where I couldn't avoid you easily and make your accusations? You think I had something to do with these men, that I'm connected to my son's fiancé's disappearance, right? You've got some nerve coming here and spewing that nonsense. You don't know what you're talking about."

"Mr. Delgado, Christine didn't run off with her personal assistant, and you know it," Grace snapped.

"That's it." Delgado rose to his feet, motioning for the maître d'. "You two have crossed a line coming here tonight. Clearly you've forgotten who you're dealing with."

The maître d' joined us, glaring daggers at Grace and I, his hands clasped in front of him. "Is there a problem here, Mr. Delgado?"

"These two are harassing me and refuse to return to their own table after I asked them to let me enjoy my meal in peace."

"I'm incredibly sorry for this inconvenience. I will see to it right away." He rounded on the two of us and snapped his fingers at us, shooing us away as if we were troublesome dogs—which was probably how he felt about us at that moment. "The two of you need to leave *immediately*. We do not tolerate this sort of behavior here at Longitude."

"Fine, we're through here anyway." I nodded my head frostily in Delgado's direction. "Have a nice night, Manny."

"You forgot your pictures," Delgado called. I turned to see him holding them by their corners as if they were something dirty that might sully his fingers.

"Keep them," I said, flashing him my teeth. "Maybe they'll help jog your memory. Oh, and Manny? Try to remember that I'm not so easily intimidated."

I didn't realize I was holding my breath until I got outside and let it out in one long burst. "So much for not being intimidated," Grace teased, handing the valet her ticket.

"Shut up," I groused. "I didn't see you being much help in there."

"Yeah, sorry. I was too busy thinking about the beef Wellington."

I patted her shoulder comfortingly. "Well, since we got kicked out of the restaurant, you're going to have to settle for microwave pizza bites at my place."

The valet returned with the Jeep and we started the drive back to my place. At the first red light Grace turned to me with an expectant look in her eyes. I was instantly suspicious. "What are you looking at me like that for?"

"I believe you agreed to have a sit-down with your parents."

"What, you want me to go right now?"

"No. Don't be stupid. I want you to call them and arrange it. What if they've decided you don't want to meet with them and have planned to go back home?"

"What a shame that would be," I deadpanned.

"Gabe—" Grace started, and I could tell that she was about to get into her lecture mode and I did *not* want to endure one of those.

"Okay, okay. But you've got to call Jin."

Grace sputtered nonsensically for a moment before she finally found her words. "What does that have to do with anything?"

"I'm tired of you going to pieces around him. Just ask him on an actual date instead of doing this—whatever it is you're doing. Think of this as me trying to help you out."

Grace drummed her fingers on the steering wheel as the light turned green. "I'll do it. But you call your parents now."

"I'll call after you call Jin," I countered.

At the next stop light, Grace pulled out her cell phone and dialed Jin's number. She did a good job hiding it, but I could see that she was nervous. After a moment she spoke, and her voice was in that almost-falsetto range that made me cringe. I motioned for her to lower her voice.

"Hey, Jin, it's Grace. I was calling to see if you want to go out with me. On a date, I mean. Yeah. Just, uh, let me know." She hung up quickly. "There. It's done. What's with that smirk?"

"You asked him on a date over voicemail? Is he even going to *check* his voicemail?"

"Hey, that's not the point here. I asked. Now call your parents."

"God, you're pushy tonight." I pulled out my phone and found the number my mother used to call me with the Hawaiian area code.

I prayed they didn't pick up so I could put this whole thing behind me, but I knew I didn't have that luck. My mother answered on the third ring.

"Hello?"

I was silent for a beat, and she repeated the greeting. I cleared my throat, shifting in the seat. "Hello, Mother."

"Gabriel?" The surprise in her voice was clear. She hadn't expected me to call her. That made two of us. "Is everything all right?"

"Everything's fine," I assured her, though I honestly doubted she was all that concerned. "Listen, I've been thinking. I was rude to you before. I sent you away without hearing you out, and I'm sorry. I want to meet up with you and give you the chance."

"Oh, thank you so much." I was put off from hearing my mother sound so relieved; it wasn't something I could recall ever hearing in her voice before. "Can we meet tomorrow?"

Tomorrow? That was really soon. I wasn't in any way ready for that. "Uh, I'm really busy tomorrow," I said quickly, pointedly ignoring the look that I was certain Grace was sending my way. "How about—how about the day after?" That was too soon for me, too, but at this point it was better than the very next day.

"Okay. Should we come to your place?"

"No, no! Why don't we meet at your hotel? I've never seen it. I'm assuming it has a nice restaurant. Let's just meet there around noon."

"Okay, we'll be there," Mother said. "Don't—" She stopped herself from saying whatever it was going to be, but if I had to guess, I would have said it was going to be *don't be late*—tardiness being one of my mother's pet peeves. Instead she finished with, "Have a good night."

I hung up and leaned back against the seat, feeling like I'd just navigated a minefield with a blindfold on.

"That wasn't so bad, was it?"

"Shut up."

We sat in silence, both of us lost in our thoughts until we pulled into the parking lot of my condo. "Well, good night," I said, getting out and closing the door behind me.

Grace rolled her window down. "Wait, what about the pizza bites?"

"You shouldn't have pressed your luck on the phone call."

Chapter Eleven

THOUGH IT SEEMED we'd hit another roadblock in the investigation, I went to work the next morning more motivated than ever. I'd seen Delgado's body language, the way he'd reacted when the pictures were put down in front of him. There was something there, and all we needed was one more connection. The answer was within reach, if we could figure that out.

Grace seemed to have the same feeling when she came in as I was flipping through the mail, perched on the edge of Mrs. Neidermeyer's desk. She actually had a big smile on her face.

"Good morning. How were your pizza bites?"

"Left frozen in the freezer where they belong," I replied, tossing several pieces of junk mail in the trash. I really wanted to toss the next piece I came to, as well, but it was sort of important, seeing as it was our light bill.

"Oh? Was there another option?"

"Maka had Chinese food ready and waiting for me at home."

Grace tilted her head contemplatively. "I don't know if that's sweet or sad. On the one hand, he had dinner for you. On the other, he knew we were going to be kicked out."

"He does know us so well, doesn't he?"

Grace chuckled. "I'm glad you find this amusing."

I tore opened the bill and examined it. No surprises, it was roughly the same as it always is. "If you can't laugh at yourself, who can you laugh at?"

"So where do we go from here?" Grace asked, slipping into Mrs. Neidermeyer's empty chair. "Maybe get Maka to see if any identification on these guys comes up?"

"I don't feel comfortable using my connection to Maka like that," I admitted. "Maybe we could find another police officer connection—one who I'm not sleeping with."

"Are you sleeping with more than one?"

"I walked into that. I also think that we should try to keep pressing—"

Grace's phone ringing cut my sentence short. "Sorry," she said, looking at the screen. She didn't answer it immediately, just stared at it with a sort of frightened look in her eyes.

"What's wrong?" I asked, concerned. I looked over her shoulder and saw it was Jin calling. "Aren't you going to answer? Wait—is this because of the voicemail? You're nervous about his answer?"

Grace just growled at me before answering the phone. "Grace Park," she said, trying her best to sound business-like, though I personally thought she sounded ridiculous. "Yeah, no it's okay. It was kind of late... Uh huh? Really?" Her face lit up and I hoped she was getting good news from Jin. "Sounds good! No, not last minute at all. It's fine."

So she was getting a date. I was really glad. That gladness faltered somewhat when her eyes suddenly bugged out. I got a bad feeling that she was about to panic.

"Actually, you know what, I made plans with Gabe tonight. I feel bad cancelling."

What are you doing? I mouthed, waving frantically at her. This wasn't a case of crashing and burning, but of the pilot forcing the plane into a dive. Had anyone ever self-sabotaged themselves so blatantly?

Just when I thought it couldn't get worse, I heard Grace's next words. "You know what, why don't we make it a double date? That way I don't have to back out."

I'm going to kill you, I mouthed, making sure she saw just how angry I was. Grace pretended I wasn't there.

"Great. Okay, I'll see you tonight. Bye."

"*What is wrong with you*?" I cried when she ended the call. "What was that?"

"I don't know! I panicked!" Grace plopped down on the couch, head in her hands. "I thought about being alone with him and freaked out. What if I make an ass out of myself?"

"You mean like you just did?"

"I'm being serious here!" Grace whined, genuinely looking like she was on the edge of distress. "I can't seem to get anything right with him, Gabe. I feel like this is my last chance. If I fuck it up now, I'm going to just call it quits."

"I don't know where my friend went," I said, sitting down next to her. "You got this. You have got to get back to feeling comfortable around him. What made you all weird?"

"I don't know. I guess the potential of something potentially happening got into my head. I'm overthinking it. I really like this guy, not like a lot of the other guys I've been with. This isn't just attraction—I mean, there's definitely attraction, like I see him and it gets—"

"I get the picture. So you like him way more than everyone else, so it's making you nervous. That's why I'm saying get back to being just friends. Stop thinking about what you *want* to be and focus on what you *are*."

"I know, I know. And I will, really. That's why I want you to be there so you can kick me under the table to help me be on track."

"I don't feel comfortable being your babysitter." I could think of a hundred things I'd rather do instead—like shave my scrotum with a straight razor.

"If you do this for me, I'll stop complaining about Mrs. Neidermeyer."

I blinked. "Wow, you're really serious about this, if you're willing to let Mrs. Neidermeyer go."

"I'll even be nice to her."

"Okay, okay, fine. I'll do it." I didn't want to see her sink any lower. "Well, I'm okay with it," I amended after a moment's thought. "I can't say for sure that Maka will agree to it."

"You have to convince him," she said forcefully. "Tell him I'll never ask another favor from him."

"We both know that won't be true. But I'll try. Maka's a nice guy, he'll probably say yes anyway."

"NO," MAKA SAID flatly as soon as I explained the situation to him. "There's no way in hell I'm doing that." Maka sat on my couch, staring at ESPN. His voice hadn't changed, but there was a stubborn set to his jaw, and I knew that getting him to change his mind would be difficult.

"Babe, you're the one who arranged a party in order to get the two of them together," I reminded him, sitting on the couch and rubbing his shoulder and bicep with one hand, as if I could massage away his recalcitrance.

"Yeah, but tagging along with them on their date to chaperone seems a little...I don't know, weird." He reached up and took my hand, pulling it away from his bicep and holding it in his own.

"If we don't go, Grace will probably cancel," I told him, snuggling closer.

"She's a big girl, she can make her own choices," Maka said, unmoved.

I decided that making the plea about Grace wasn't going to get me anywhere. Sure, Maka liked Grace, but me, he—well he *really* liked me. A switch up of tactics was best.

I began to stroke the hand that held mine with my free hand the way I knew he liked. "Grace is my best friend in the world. I really want her to be happy. She really likes Jin, which is why she's being such a freak."

"I understand that," Maka said cautiously, like he could sense my intention and was waiting for the blow to fall.

"If we do this and it works out, then it's a win-win. Grace is happy, I won't be worried about her anymore, *and* she'll make my life easier by not complaining about Mrs. Neidermeyer."

Maka gave me a long look down his nose. "You really want me to do this?" I nodded, waiting to pull out the puppy dog eyes, I didn't want to waste them on him if he wasn't going to be resistant. "Fine. But whether it works out well for them or not, this is the last time."

"Agreed. If she can't pull it off this time, she's on her own."

Maka pulled me in for a sudden kiss, which I wasn't ashamed to admit caught me off guard.

"What was that for?"

"For being such a good friend. You're an incredibly caring guy, you know that."

I shrugged, looking away from him, embarrassed by his words. Taking a compliment had never exactly been my forte, especially in a relationship; Trevor had never given them, seemed to go out of his way to avoid them, in fact.

"If you say so."

Maka gently took my chin and tilted my head until I was looking into his eyes once again. "I do."

Heat spread through my body under the intensity of his gaze, my fingertips tingled. I knew it was cheesy, but I didn't know if I would ever get used to the way I felt when he looked at me like that.

"How much time do you think we have?" Maka asked me even as he guided me across his lap so I was straddling him.

I grinned, leaning down to cover Maka's mouth with my own, saying, "Enough, I hope," just before our lips met.

Unfortunately, the universe—or Grace—conspired against us. We'd barely begun kissing before Grace messaged me the location of the restaurant Jin chose and the time. Though I could see he didn't want to stop, Maka didn't complain when we had to get ready, and five minutes before seven, he and I stood in front of the restaurant waiting for Grace and Jin.

"I really hope that Grace controlled herself when dressing for this date tonight," I said while keeping an eye on the parking lot. "If we have a repeat of that outfit she wore to the dinner party, I don't think there's any hope for her."

"We'll see," Maka said, though it sounded like in his mind there might already be no hope.

I wasn't ready to give up on Grace yet, though. There was so much between those two it seemed plain to me that they were wild about each other.

True, Jin hadn't come out and said it, but to still put up with her crazy, especially when our business nearly got him killed not too long ago? There *had* to be some reason. I could only hope that Jin returned her feelings.

He said yes to the date, though, so that was a good sign.

"There they are." Jin and Grace approached from the parking lot. It didn't take a body language expert to see that they were still feeling uncomfortable together; their shoulders were tight, and they kept giving each other sidelong looks.

Grace had at least dressed sensibly, so one of my concerns was gone. Instead of an over the top dress she wore well-fitting designer jeans and a nice low-cut blouse in a pastel blue that highlighted her sun-darkened skin.

"How did you get here before us?" Grace asked in greeting. "Did you use your siren?"

"I was born on the island; I don't need to use a siren to beat a Mainlander." Grace scowled at the word *Mainlander* as if it were a pejorative.

I wasn't going to get in the middle of their little competitive streak by pointing out that Maka had definitely exceeded the speed limit on the way there. Instead, ever the diplomat, I said, "Let's go in and get our table."

Jin had chosen a nice restaurant—though not quite the caliber of Longitude—that was famous for a fusion of Greek and Hawaiian food. The environment was nice and relaxed, each table providing the expected amount of privacy for a restaurant.

The waiter arrived right on the heels of the hostess, a big smile on his face. "Can I start you off with drinks?"

"I'm driving," Jin said before ordering a glass of iced tea, Maka following suit.

Grace looked torn for a moment as she stared at the menu, biting her lower lip.

Jin picked up on her frustration and put a hand on her shoulder—a gesture I was pleased to note. "I don't mind if you have a drink."

Grace gave him a shy smile and turned to the waiter. "I'll have a glass of chardonnay."

I actually had no intention of drinking tonight, but Grace gave me a look that clearly said *Don't make me drink alone*, so I echoed her order.

The waiter left and an awkward silence descended on the table for a moment. Not wanting to let it get its hooks in and make things worse, I attempted to start a conversation. "What do you two have planned for tonight?"

"Well, dinner, obviously," Grace said unnecessarily.

"Anything else?"

Jin shrugged. "Actually, I hadn't thought about what might come later. I figured let's see how the night goes."

Not a bad answer, all things considered.

"So how's work going?" Maka asked, doing his best to keep the conversation going with me.

"Pretty good," Jin answered, taking a drink of his water as he perused the menu. "These two keep me busy, and the cases they bring me, I'm never bored."

"Yeah," Maka said wryly, squeezing my knee under the table. "Sometimes I think they're *too* exciting."

"Well, it's yet to be something we can't handle," I said modestly.

"Actually, I was thinking about this one," Jin said excitedly. "We've looked at maps of the locations, but that's not necessarily enough, right? You've been to Delgado's office, you've been to the airport. Why don't you visit the middle location?"

"You mean the warehouse?" Grace asked, sounding intrigued.

"Yeah. Maybe there's security cameras nearby or something that we can hack into." He realized the illegality of his words and glanced sheepishly at Maka. "Sorry."

"I didn't hear anything," Maka said, looking around like he wasn't paying attention. "But seriously, though, I don't think that's a very good idea."

"Yes, it is," Grace said, eyes lighting up. "We don't have enough stuff yet to really make Delgado squirm. But if we can get access to camera footage and it has something on it, then we can use that to actually have leverage over him. It's a huge opportunity."

"Delgado is dangerous. He's proven that already," Maka argued, frown deepening. He was no doubt thinking about Delgado's assistant's attempts on my life—without a doubt at Delgado's bidding.

I felt bad for being the source of so much worry for him, but I couldn't live in a bubble, and I had a job to do. "That's why I really want to take that schmuck down."

Maka couldn't argue with me there, I knew, and manipulating him like that was yet another thing I could feel a little bad for.

"We'll be careful," I added, trying to make him feel better about the plan.

"Considering how much crap still happens to you when you're careful, I'm not sure that comforts me."

"He has a point," Grace piped up, unnecessarily.

The waiter interrupted the flow of conversation then to take our orders and deliver our drinks. Before we could get back onto a topic that would just annoy Maka or make him worry more, I decided to take control of the conversation.

"So, Jin, what are your hobbies outside of the computery things you do for Grace and I?"

"I like watching old movies," Jin admitted, as if the topic might be embarrassing.

Grace, however, perked right up. "Really? Me too. What kind of old movies do you like?"

"I'm a big Hitchcock fan." Jin had gained a bit of confidence now that it was clear his interest wasn't going to be rebuked or mocked, it seemed. He also couldn't have picked a better topic, not with Grace.

"*Me too*! I actually took an entire class devoted to studying Hitchcock films."

"Have you seen *Young and Innocent*?"

"Three or four times! I love the way circumstances conspire in the story just right. The tension is crazy. Have you seen *The Lady Vanishes*?"

Jin grinned. "You're the first person I've met who's actually seen it!"

They conversed about the various films of Alfred Hitchcock as the waiter brought our food and through most of the dinner itself, basically forgetting that we were there. Not that I was complaining.

Maka and I shared a pleased look. Things had taken an unexpected turn for the better with the two of them. With any luck Grace would be past her awkwardness now that the ice was so thoroughly broken by the Hitchcock talk.

"You're a genius," Maka said, leaning in close to me and whispering in my ear.

"I know," I replied, winking.

"Think it's time?" I nodded. Maka cleared his throat, drawing Grace and Jin's attention back to us. "All right, guys, we're done. This has been really fun, but we need to get going. I've got early watch tomorrow."

"Okay," Grace said brightly. There was a sparkle in her eyes that had been gone for a while, replaced by her own constant mortification. Her cheeks were flushed with more than just white wine. "See you at work tomorrow, Gabe. Have a good night, Maka."

"Good night," Jin said, giving us both the typical manly and brusque head-nod farewell. Maka called the waiter over and we got our half of the bill. As we were leaving the restaurant I looked back toward Grace. Once I was sure Jin wasn't looking, I gave her a thumbs up. She mouthed *Thank you*, and I left the restaurant feeling like I'd done my good deed for the month.

Well, if Grace could manage not to screw it up.

Chapter Twelve

GRACE WAS IN a much better mood when she met me at work the next morning, with an ear-to-ear grin I'd been missing from her lately.

"Well, someone is in a good mood today," I said, letting a small amount of suggestiveness slip into my voice.

"Why wouldn't I be? It's a beautiful day."

I looked up at the sky skeptically. It was overcast, and the wind smelled of rain. "A beautiful day, huh? Did you and Jin hit any more snags after we left?"

"Nope." Together we walked into the office where Mrs. Neidermeyer sat in her usual place. "You reminded me that I didn't need to act so weird with him. When you asked the question that led to Hitchcock, I just let myself relax."

Mrs. Neidermeyer decided to join in the conversation then. "Didn't make a fool of yourself on this date, huh?"

Grace opened her mouth quickly and then closed it. I wondered if she was remembering the conditions on which I'd agreed to make it a second date. Instead of a sharp retort of any kind she simply said, "No, not this time. I guess it's a miracle."

Mrs. Neidermeyer made a noise that was difficult to describe. "Well, it's about time you got your act together and started acting like you had some sense in your head."

Grace and I both just stared at her, floored. What the hell was that? I understood why Grace was being nice—she really didn't have a choice, at least for a little while until she decided that she'd paid enough for my company on the date and went back to the way things had been.

But Mrs. Neidermeyer? That was a mystery. Maybe they'd changed her medication.

"Uh, thanks...I think?"

"You've got no appointments this morning, since I know you weren't going to ask," she said, going right back to her normal self.

"Good," said Grace, her voice only slightly frosty. "We're going out. We've got work to do."

"I might be gone by the time you get back. I've got to leave early. I'm trying out naughty cooking tonight and I have some things I need to get ready."

I cringed. "Whatever you say, Mrs. Neidermeyer. And in the future, feel free to just stop at the leaving early part. The details aren't really necessary."

We hurried out, partly because we wanted to escape before Mrs. Neidermeyer decided to clue us in to what might be involved in naughty cooking, but mostly because we were eager to get something more that we could wield against Delgado, anything that might prove his involvement.

I drove this time, my great familiarity with my GPS coming in handy. Grace didn't even own one, so we would have had no chance of finding the place in her Jeep.

The road to the warehouse was fairly direct, so even I would have no trouble finding it. It was in an industrial area along the coast, not too far from Waikiki beach. The buildings were mostly old and weather-worn, having endured plenty of rough seasons in their day. They were nothing more than tall concrete slabs, windowless and free of any sort of adornments other than faded signs that announced the names of companies.

I slowed down once we neared our destination, keeping an eye out for Dostavka on any of the buildings.

"I think this is the place," Grace said uncertainly, pointing across my chest out of my window. I could understand her lack of confidence in that; it was a gated off space, but there was nothing there behind the gate but a few stacked cargo containers, all of them open. It honestly looked like no one had been near there in years.

It certainly didn't look like the sort of place Christine Hu would have ended up.

Grace had the same thoughts. "Why the hell would Christine come here?"

"I'm coming up blank on that front too." I pulled the car into a small parking lot next to the building.

"Do you think maybe she didn't come here of her own free will?"

"We can't really dismiss any idea right now," I said, killing the engine. "All we know is the car was here. Maybe she was driving, maybe she wasn't. Let's look around and see if we can see any cameras."

"Would be kind of a waste of money to have cameras at this place," Grace said, but she got out of the car with me. We only had access to one side of the space's perimeter, the rest of it being blocked off by water and other buildings. The only real security we could see was the padlocked fence with the ringlets of barbed wire across the top.

I craned my neck to see as much of the space as I could, but I didn't see any sign of security cameras. "Looks like it's pretty barren. Nothing for Jin to hack into. Another dead end."

"Yeah, and every dead end seems to be painting a less than happy picture for Christine. There's no way that any circumstances that brought her *here* were good."

I leaned against the driver's side door of my car, arms crossed, index finger of my right hand tapping steadily against my bicep as my thoughts raced, trying to assemble what we knew into something useful. "We have no security cameras to tap into, so we're going to get nowhere with that angle. We have no idea what went on here, and no way to find out. I highly doubt anyone involved is going to go blabbing about it."

"Maybe knowing about the place is enough to rattle Delgado?"

"I doubt it. He seems pretty unshakeable. We need something more than circumstantial evidence." An idea hit me, and I pulled open the car door. "If we can dig up a connection between Delgado and the company that owns this place, maybe that will be enough to finally knock him off his game. Let's go."

I sped a little bit on the way back to the office. My gut told me this was going to point us in the right direction.

A black Range Rover was parked in one of the parking spaces in front of the office when I pulled the car in, and a man stood beside the driver's side door, wearing a fancy suit. Thanks to all of our dealings with Delgado, suits were beginning to lose their appeal to me.

"I don't like the looks of this," I muttered, unbuckling and slowly getting out of the car.

The man was perfunctory and business-like in his tone, and he wasted no time. "Are you Grace Park and Gabriel Maxfield?"

"We are. What's this about?"

The man pulled a folded piece of paper out of his inner jacket pocket and handed it to me. "I'm officially serving you with a restraining order on behalf of Manuel Delgado."

I stared at him dumbly as he pulled out a clipboard and passed it to me for my signature. I signed it mechanically, mind still glued on the words *restraining order* as they bounced around in my head again and again and again.

Once my signature was on the paper the man turned on his heel without saying anything else and returned to his Range Rover.

"Well," Grace said, taking the restraining order and unfolding it, "that was unexpected." I nodded, still unable to find my voice. "I think it's a good thing, though. Right? I mean, he went out of his way to tell us to stay away from him. That must mean we've got him flustered, right?"

Grace's words helped me shake the stupor that had settled over me. She was right. Of course she was.

"We've got him on the run," I agreed. "Now let's get inside and find something that we can finally use to nail his ass."

"Woah not so fast," Grace told me, grabbing my shoulder before I could move.

I shook free of her hand. "What's the problem? We're wasting time."

"You've got to get moving if you want to meet your parents. You told them noon, right?"

I snorted. "I think taking down Manuel Delgado is more important than keeping a lunch date with my parents."

I started for the office again and again she grabbed me. "Hey, I kept my end of the bargain. You have to keep yours."

"That's not fair! You got to have a date with a hot guy. *I* get stuck with my parents."

Grace shrugged, unmoved. "Not my fault you entered into an uneven bargain of your own making."

"What about Delgado?" I demanded, clinging to the hope that the job would get me out of this meeting.

"You'll be gone what, an hour at most? I can handle the research until you get back. Just go. You never know when this opportunity will present itself again."

"Fine," I grumbled, seeing Grace wasn't going to cave on this one. "I'll be back in one hour tops."

I personally didn't think I'd last ten minutes, but there was no need to say that aloud.

THE AQUA PALMS hotel was without a doubt a luxury hotel, but it wasn't quite up to the standards I expected for my parents. It was a lavish building, surrounded by a lot of palm trees. It looked like something that would be used as an establishing shot for a stereotypically Hawai'ian television show or movie.

My parents were waiting for me just inside the doors. To the right behind them was the hotel's first floor lounge. They stood their stiffly and awkwardly, and I guess I couldn't blame them after the way I greeted them the last time. There was no door to slam in their face this time, though, and at least I showed up.

To be honest, though, I'd considered not. I could have made up some nonsense to tell Grace about it and just sit in my car somewhere for an hour, or get lunch. I don't know why I didn't take that option, to be honest. Standing in front of my parents, all stiff and prim as always, I regretted my choice.

"Hello, Gabe," my father said stiffly. My mother went in for an awkward hug—very unlike her—and the only reason I didn't jerk out of her reach on instinct is that it caught me off guard.

"Since when are we a hugging family?" I asked in an effort to break the tension. My mother laughed nervously and my father's lips stretched into what might have been a smile or a sign of gastrointestinal distress.

I was surprised when they led me not toward the lounge but toward the elevator. "Where are we going?" I asked uncertainly.

"We figured maybe my room would be a good place for us to talk," Mother replied. "It's quieter and it has a nice view of the area from its balcony."

I didn't relish the thought of going upstairs with them, but then I realized that this would cut down on the time we were together. We wouldn't be obligated to order food and thus wouldn't have to wait until it came. We could get this over with.

"Well, lead the way."

We were silent in the elevator as it made its way up to the twelfth floor. It was like having flashbacks to my childhood, and the way things were any time we traveled together. A silence that was as oppressive and abusive as shouting. The things unsaid could hurt as much as the things that were. My family was incapable of having a conversation that didn't somehow center on manipulations or criticisms.

I really should go.

The thought echoed like firework cannons in my mind, louder each time. I could do it; just reach the twelfth floor, tell them I made a mistake, turn around and head back to work. The only thing that kept me from doing so was the thought that they might think it was about *them*, might take it as a victory, and I flat-out refused to give them any sort of victory. I would suffer through this if it killed me.

The room that they led me to wasn't as lavish as I'd expected, either. Oh, it was nice, but not the hotel's best, clearly. Instead of a suite it was a simple room—well, a simple room that had a door that led out to a beautiful, private, balcony.

"It's a beautiful room," I said politely, tired of the weight of the silence.

"Isn't it?" Mother replied. There it was, her trained civility coming out of its own accord. Mother was the master of the art of meaningless conversation, wielding pleasantries the way a marksman wielded a gun. "Your father's is one floor up. It's just as nice."

That gave me pause. What did she mean that my father's room was one floor up? It struck me then that down in the lobby she'd said *my room*, not *our room*. I looked around the room, searching for evidence of their presence. There, on the bedside table—the right side of the bed, which my mother always slept in, for as long as I could remember—was a book, one of the latest self-help craze books. Without a doubt my mother's.

There was not one sign that my father had ever been in that room before this moment to be found. What was going on?

"Why are the two of you in separate rooms?" I asked, just like they wanted me to. The comments might have seem casually dropped, but in reality, they were bait, carefully laid down to lure me in, though I couldn't guess what the purpose would be at this point.

There was something, though. There always was.

"Your mother and I are divorced." There was my father, with his legendary lack of tact. He'd always been a blunt man, one of the only traits of his I actually somewhat admired. "Have been for four years."

I tried to summon some of the emotion I was sure I was expected to feel in that moment, but came up empty. Didn't people feel some sort of loss at the end of their parents' marriage?

"You don't look surprised," said my father, a note of challenge in his voice.

"Let's go outside on the balcony," Mother said, touching my father's arm. "It's such lovely weather today."

"If you say so." The sky was looking more like rain with each passing hour. But sure, lovely. The power of my mother's ability to deflect was astounding.

Outside the wind had picked up, now blowing almost constantly. The palm trees she spoke of—we did have a great view of them—were constantly swaying.

"Why did you get divorced?"

"I don't think there's ever just one reason," Mother said.

Father, however, was more forthcoming. "We came to realize that the reasons we had for staying together didn't seem to add up anymore."

"We came to the decision together, though," Mother said quickly. "We talked it out and decided it was the right thing to do."

"As long as you're happy," I said, the words lacking any real meaning. "What are you guys doing here? Did you come to tell me about the divorce?"

"No, we came here for you." My mother's hands clenched and unclenched, the only sign I could see that she was nervous about this. "We've wanted to reach out to you for a long time."

"Oh?" I challenged, not believing it. "What stopped you?"

"You didn't tell us where you were going," Father said, the accusation now completely unhidden in his voice.

"You didn't have a problem finding me here, did you? With all the resources you had at your disposal, I'm sure you could have found me without very much effort."

They shared a look then, before my mother spoke. "We thought you didn't want to be found. After...after everything. We thought it would be best to respect your wishes on that, for once. We even called it our graduation present to you."

"What made you change your mind?"

"Four months ago, I sold your grandfather's company."

The revelation floored me. My father had received nothing more than the company in my grandfather's will—and he'd been gunning for that his entire life. There were times I'd genuinely believed he wanted my grandfather to hurry up and die so he could take the company. Now he'd sold it?

"Why?"

"I don't have a head for business. Your grandfather knew that. He only left me the company because I begged him. And because it was the only thing he had to give me, since his estate went to you."

Yes, probably the single greatest damage to my father's ego, my receiving my grandfather's money.

"So you drove the company into the ground and then you sold it?"

"Actually, the company was doing very well—though that's due to the guidance and decisions of other people, not me. I can admit that. This was the right thing to do."

My mother's hand moved toward me, like she wanted to take mine, before moving back, rethinking her decision. "We wanted to tell you about it, but we couldn't decide if we wanted to bother you. We've had a lot of time to dwell on our mistakes. With your grandfather gone and you out of the picture, we were alone, with only each other, and we realized that we only had ourselves to blame. Then, we saw you on TV, learned you were here, and decided we had to at least reach out to you."

"What was your goal?" I asked.

"We didn't expect to even get to speak with you," Father confessed. "So I can't say we had a goal beyond seeing you and having this talk. Now that we're here, though, I want to give you this. I know how much your grandfather meant to you."

He slid an envelope toward me. I took it and opened it, wondering what could be inside. The last thing I expected to find was a check in there for a quarter of a million dollars.

"What is this?"

"A check."

"Okay, I can see that. Why did you give it to me?"

"It's your portion of the sale of your grandfather's company."

Anger began to bubble up in me. Money. It was always money. "It was yours. I have my money from him. I don't need it. I'm set. You can take this back."

"You're turning this down?"

"Why do you sound so surprised? Everything comes down to money with you. It always does." I rose to my feet, unwilling to handle this.

"Can't you see we're trying?" Mother burst out. The actual show of emotion is what stopped me in my tracks more than the words. "We'll admit that we made a lot of mistakes. We're not going to deny it."

"You made everything in my life about money," I said, voice shaking. Maybe I *was* glad I came, so I could finally say this to them. "You reduced everything, right down to my worth as your son, to money."

"I don't think that—"

"That's why I left in the first place," I reminded my mother before she could say anything more. "You made it clear you had no use for me when I wouldn't give you access to my inheritance. Everything with you is about control. I'm not going to take your check with all the strings that are attached to it."

"We know we made mistakes in the past, but that doesn't mean we can't change. We want to apologize."

"And you thought money was the way to do it?"

"That is separate," Father said shortly. "Your grandfather would have wanted you to have the money. We wanted to honor that."

"You didn't do much honoring of him when he was alive," I said, but even I thought it was in poor taste.

Father bristled. "Our relationship was complicated."

"That's something I understand," I said, and for the first time, my anger lagged. I stood there for a moment, indecision paralyzing me. The choice was a subconscious one, at first, and then I made my way to the small table on the balcony and sat back down.

"I don't know what you want from me," I said tiredly.

"We want a chance," Mother almost whispered.

"How much can happen in one sitting?"

A hopeful look came over my mother's face. "We're not foolish enough to think that we're going to mend everything today. But it would be enough to know whether or not there's a chance."

Was there, though? Sure, they'd come to Hawai'i for me, but that was hardly a sweeping gesture. Hawai'i was beautiful, and it wouldn't be that hard for them to get away. But they *were* here. Did that mean something?

I looked at their faces, and I looked at the check on the table. If I thought about it, maybe it *was* a bigger gesture than I'd considered. They'd spent so long trying to get money from me, for them to now be giving this to me, maybe it was meant as a sign that their values had changed, that their priorities had shifted. My money wasn't the point anymore.

Maybe I was.

"I can't say yes, not with any certainty," I said, realizing I'd been staring at them for what must have been at least two minutes.

"Would you at least be willing to see us one more time before we leave Friday afternoon?" Father asked, negotiating like a businessman.

Was this a road I wanted to go down? My parents had caused me pretty much nothing but misery for as long as I could remember. I didn't owe them anything.

I thought about Grace and her situation with her parents. She wanted to mend things, and they didn't, and look how it left her hurt. Maybe I owed myself something, if not them. I needed closure on this as much as Grace did, judging by the way their past actions continued to affect me even after so long.

"I'll do my best," I replied at last, and my parents visibly relaxed. "I've got an important case going on, so I won't make any promises, but I'll try."

"Thank you." Mother reached out for my hand. I didn't know what to do; I didn't pull back, but nor did I return her squeeze. I didn't let the touch linger, either. I pulled my hand away as quickly as I could without it seeming rude.

"Okay," I said, clearing my throat. "I've got to get back to work."

Mother frowned. "You haven't had anything to eat yet!"

"I know, but I promised Grace I wouldn't be too long. Like I said, we're working a big case."

"Is it dangerous?"

The question caught me off guard for a moment as did the genuine concern in her voice. "Uh, well, it's less dangerous than other jobs I've done."

BY THE TIME I reached Paradise Investigations again, it was nearing two o'clock and a light rain had begun to fall. I didn't mind the rain; I'd grown so used to it in Seattle that I found its lower frequency in Hawai'i to be a little sad. I always found my mood lifting when it finally fell.

I cut the engine and rested my head on the steering wheel, eyes closed, soaking in the silence and the steadily growing sound of the rain beating a tempo against my car. I wasn't ready to go inside and face Grace and what I knew would be six thousand questions about how my meeting with my parents went. I needed to get my own thoughts together before I could talk about them with anyone else.

I gathered as much strength as I could from the silence, letting it infuse me with its calm. That calm was shattered by the rapping of someone's knuckles against my window.

I jumped, ready to turn an angry scowl on Grace, but it wasn't her standing at my window. It was one of the two burly men I'd been seeing around. Their faces were blank, impossible to read, but a menacing aura radiated off them that even the most oblivious of people would have been able to sense.

The closer one, the one with the ponytail, captured my gaze with his own and held it prisoner as surely as if he'd grabbed it in his hands. The last thing I wanted to do was get out of the car, but I also couldn't just sit huddled frightened in my car. Driving away wasn't an option either.

There was nothing for it but to get out of the car and face these assholes down. I pushed the car door open, forcing Ponytail back. When I spoke, I did my best to keep my voice steady. "Can I help you gentlemen?"

"You've been a rather busy man," Slicked Hair said. There was a hint of an accent in his voice, but I couldn't place it exactly.

"That's what happens when you have a job," I said dryly.

"You've visited some strange places too," Ponytail added. "Places that you've no business going. What is it you could be looking for, I wonder?"

"Well, that would be between me and whoever I work for, now wouldn't it?"

Ponytail chuckled darkly. "I understand you're new to the island, Mr. Maxfield, so let me give you some advice."

"I'm not in the habit of taking advice from strangers," I said, stepping around him. Slicked Hair moved into my path, his face remaining as blank as it had been before.

"Hear us out," Ponytail said. "It might come in handy in the future."

A car pulled into the parking lot, tires squealing as it came to a stop beside us. Maka, his face stony and hard, climbed out of the car, leaving it running.

Ponytail and Slicked Hair looked Maka over from head to toe and then shared a look.

"I see now is a bad time," Ponytail said, lip rising in the slightest of sneers. "We will continue this conversation another time, I'm sure, Mr. Maxfield."

With one last look at Maka, Ponytail and Slicked Hair walked away, heading down the road toward where their car was no doubt parked.

"What's going on?" Grace called from the office door. "I heard a car...who are—is that...?" Grace pointed toward the two men and I nodded.

"Yup. Our two mystery photo men. I've seen them around a lot, too."

"You have?" The question came out of Maka like a bark, his police detective voice. "When?"

I told Maka about the multiple sightings I'd had, and how they were in every photo, while a voice in the back of my head whispered, *I should have told him right away.*

"Why the hell didn't you say something?" Maka demanded, fury deepening his voice.

"I didn't want you to worry," I said, uncomfortable having this argument in front of Grace. "You're always getting nervous about this job, and the last thing I thought you needed was more stress—"

"That's not fair," he interrupted, though he didn't sound quite as angry. "Don't say it was about me. You just didn't want me to worry so you didn't have to hear me worry."

I opened my mouth to argue, but stopped, because he wasn't entirely wrong. "Maybe," I said instead. "But you don't like it when I worry about you in your job, and your job is more dangerous than mine."

"In normal circumstances, yes. But this is you, Gabe, and you have a tendency to walk into bad shit. Like those guys."

"Who were they?" Grace interjected, and I was grateful for the distraction.

I thought Maka would ignore her question, but after several beats he turned to her. "I've seen their faces before, though I don't know their names. I know they're suspected to have connections to the Russian mafia on the island."

Suddenly the accent came to me. It was definitely Eastern European.

"People have always whispered that Delgado was dirty," Grace reasoned, mind turned to the case once more. "This verifies that."

Maka frowned. "Does it?"

I nodded. "Think about it. Delgado's future daughter-in-law goes missing. There are these Russian mafia-affiliated people turning up all over the place where she's at, and where we are when we investigate her disappearance. Delgado's clearly involved with the Russian mafia."

"So why target Christine?"

That one took several minutes for me to think out. "Well, she ended up at the place, Dostavka. Sounds Eastern European, right? Maybe it's a front for them."

"She went there from Delgado's office," Grace added, hopping aboard my train of thought. "Maybe she followed Sergio or Manuel there and saw something that she shouldn't have?"

Maka made a noise low in his throat. "That's a bit of a stretch."

"My gut tells me Grace is right. The more we put together, the more it makes sense. We went to that place today, and they knew it. They said, 'You've visited some strange places today.' Combine that with the restraining order Delgado filed against us—"

"Delgado filed a restraining order?" Maka repeated.

"—and it all adds up to a very uneasy Delgado. We're on to something here."

"Delgado got a restraining order?" Maka repeated. "Guys, that's serious."

"It's because he knew we were close after we confronted him with those pictures," Grace said, waving away Maka's concern like it was no big deal. "Now that we know who they are, we've got him. This is what we needed to finally get some answers."

"Are you two even listening to me?" Maka cried.

"Yes, we are," I assured him. "But I honestly think Grace is right, Maka. And if she is, then we might finally be able to find out what happened to Christine Hu. We owe that to her mother."

"I agree that they need answers, but you two always do this. You go running half-cocked into god knows what. You do remember the last time you tangled with Delgado you nearly ended up dead like five times?"

"It was three," I corrected, though I could see his point. "Listen, Maka, I promise we'll be careful. But we've got to take this to Delgado and force him to answer."

"He has a restraining order on you," Maka protested. "You could go to jail."

"He's not going to call the police. It's a bluff that he hopes frightens us. But it's not going to work. Come on, Grace. Let's pay Manny a visit."

"If you end up arrested, I'm not getting you out," Maka said indignantly.

"Yes, you will," I said, kissing him on the cheek. I opened the door and slid behind the wheel before the thought struck me. "Maka, what are you doing here, by the way? Not that I'm not extremely grateful you came, but...why?"

"I knew you had your meeting with your parents today, and I thought you might need cheering up, so I came by to check on you."

"Aww." Such a sweet gesture, reminding me again how lucky I was that I had him in my life. "You're such a great guy, Maka. I'll tell you about my parents when I get home."

"If you're not arrested," he corrected.

"Don't worry, I'll use my one phone call to tell you about it."

Chapter Thirteen

DESPITE MY CASUAL demeanor, I grew more nervous as we approached Delgado's office building. Maka wasn't wrong; there was a definite chance Delgado would call the cops. Or worse, if he felt threatened.

But we need to do this. The quicker we could catch him off guard with our knowledge the greater our chances of finding out what happened to Christine, and maybe even finding her.

Nailing Delgado's ass would be an added bonus.

The nervousness seemed to reach its crescendo as we approached the sliding glass doors of the building.

"How do you want to handle this?" Grace asked me. Her words came fast, a sign of her own nerves.

"We know what floor it is," I told her, bracing for what we needed to do. "We go in, we don't stop. Ready?"

Grace nodded, biting her lower lip.

I took a deep breath and as I exhaled, we marched purposefully through the door, long strides, crossing the room as quickly as we could. We paid no attention to the secretary behind her desk, our sights focused on the elevator.

"Excuse me," the secretary called, realizing we were bypassing her entirely. Grace sped up and opened the elevator doors. "Where do you think you're going?"

"Up," I replied. "You can either go with us or not, but we're going up." The secretary hesitated, torn. I moved to take her hand away from the elevator door and she stepped away, like she was scared I would do something. The last glimpse I had of her was of her scurrying to the desk, no doubt to notify her boss or security.

Grace hit the button for the executive floor. "There's probably going to be security there when we get there," I warned her.

"I can handle it," she said, throwing her hair back over her shoulder.

I grinned. The elevator opened onto Delgado's personal assistant, standing there, hands on her hips, looking for all the world like she wanted to shout *You shall not pass* at us.

"You're not supposed to be here. Security is on its way."

Grace gave her a cold smile. "Lovely." Without another word, she barged right past the assistant. "Manny! Get out here! We're not going anywhere!"

"She's pretty insistent," I added, sidestepping the assistant myself.

"This is completely unacceptable!" The personal assistant was all but stomping her foot now. "You cannot be up here. You don't have an appointment!"

Grace had reached Delgado's door and was banging on it in a continuous, steady rhythm. "Come on, Manny, we know you're here. Are you afraid to face us? Scared of what we know?"

Grace was an expert at pushing peoples' buttons; the door flew open then, and Manuel Delgado stood there, his face livid with rage, his nostrils flaring with each exhalation, and his teeth gritted so tightly I thought for sure I would hear them crack from the pressure.

"Just what the hell do you think you're doing? This is a place of business."

"I've called security, Mr. Delgado," the personal assistant said quickly, like she was eager to let him know she'd done something and hadn't just been standing there.

"Actually, call the police," Delgado instructed, eyes cold. "These two are violating a restraining order."

"Oh, yes, please call the police," I told her, digging into my pocket for my cell phone. "You want to use this? When they get here, I'm sure they'll be very interested in what we know about a little place owned by *Dostavka*."

Delgado's face went even whiter at the company's name. We had him. "That won't be necessary. Tell security they won't be needed, either. The two of you should come in."

"You broke a little quicker than I expected," Grace told Delgado once we were in his office with the door shut behind us.

"You're mistaking not wanting to make a scene for a victory," Delgado said, though the words lacked the strength they might have; he knew as well as we did that a victory was exactly what this was.

I wasn't about to let him keep thinking he had the upper hand, either. "We know about Dostavka, Mr. Delgado. And we know about the men you sent stalking Christine Hu, as well, so you might as well not bother lying."

"I told you before when you showed me those pictures that I have no idea who those men are," Delgado snapped.

"We didn't believe you then and we don't believe you now."

Delgado leveled a powerful glare on me, one that might have once caused me to shrink back but, now that we had him over the barrel, had little effect.

"Better men than you wouldn't dare talk to me like that."

"Maybe they're better in your eyes," I said with a shrug. "But now we know better."

"Maybe he doesn't know, Gabe. But you know what? Maybe Sergio does," Grace suggested. "We should call the police and see if they can figure out how much he does or doesn't know."

"For fuck's sake!" Delgado buried his hands in his face. "Fine. I'll tell you what you want to know. Just leave Sergio out of this."

"Tell us about those men," I prompted.

"They're enforcers for the Russian mafia."

"Yes, yes," Grace said impatiently, waving her hand for him to go on. "We know that already. Plenty of people have said you and your company are dirty, and now we know it's true."

Delgado straightened, insulted. "I had no idea who they were until a few days ago. I may be ruthless in my business dealings, but I would never risk everything I've built for myself and my children."

"Then how did they get involved?"

"That's a long and complicated story."

"We've got time."

Delgado slumped back in his chair, hand against his forehead. "When I invited Sergio into the company, he thought he needed to impress me. He financed several business ventures by borrowing money from the Russians. When they failed, he turned to laundering money to pay back his debts. Then, last year, an employee discovered it."

"Oh my God." Grace's hand rose to her mouth. "The son of the woman who hired Carrie to investigate you."

Delgado nodded slowly. "Yes," he said, his voice a hoarse whisper. "The discovery that no doubt led to his death, and certainly led to your business partner's."

"You ordered them dead to cover for your son," I accused.

"No. I wholeheartedly believe that was the Russians. I didn't know anything about this until Ashford's confession."

Grace shook her head in disgust. "Then what makes you so sure it was the Russians' doing and not your son's?"

"My son wouldn't do that. And he wouldn't have willingly endangered Christine, either. He loved her."

"So you know what happened to Christine." It wasn't a question; I knew the answer already.

Delgado rose from his chair and walked to a fully stocked bar near the large windows that looked out over the street. He poured himself a glass of scotch, downing the entire thing, before he answered.

"The night she disappeared, Sergio was going to meet the Russians, try to get more time. Christine followed him there for some reason. They knew who she was; as you pointed out, it seems they've been following her for some time now. They kidnapped her, took her to use as leverage. They were afraid that Sergio was going to vanish without paying them."

"What about Travis Brent?"

Delgado poured a second glass. If I didn't know better, I would have said that the man was feeling actual shame at that moment. "I paid him twenty thousand dollars to leave the island for a few weeks. I needed to feed the story that they'd run off together."

"Why didn't you go to the police? Why didn't Sergio?"

"Sergio was in too deep already," Delgado said bitterly, turning back to me and Grace. "He'd stolen money from this company; he'd become involved with gangsters. He isn't innocent in this, I know it."

There weren't enough words for the disgust I felt toward this man at that moment. "So you let Helena Hu suffer—let Christine suffer—to protect your son."

"Not just him! Do you think these men would hesitate to kill Christine the moment the police or the feds became involved?"

He had a point there. Men didn't become enforcers for the mafia if they had scruples. Delgado was right about that, at least. These men no doubt viewed Christine as a useful bargaining tip and nothing more. The moment she lost her usefulness they would discard her.

"And what exactly are you and your son doing while your future daughter-in-law—well, ex future daughter-in-law, probably—is in the hands of the fucking *Russian mafia*?" Grace demanded, stalking toward Delgado.

Delgado actually cowered at her approach. How the mighty had fallen.

"We're working on getting the money together. We're almost finished, one more day and we'll have it. We'll pay them the money and they'll return Christine, safe and relatively sound."

"How do you know they'll hand her over?" I asked, feeling like it was an obvious question he was overlooking in his eagerness to be sure that his son didn't get in trouble.

"They will!" Delgado sounded almost wild in his insistence. His eyes bugged out a little as he spoke. "They want their money."

I shook my head disdainfully. "I thought you were a smarter man than that. As soon as they get their money, they're going to kill her. She's a loose thread. I'm not a mafia expert, but I'm pretty sure they don't like loose threads."

"They won't!" His insistence revealed just how desperate Delgado had become. "If they kill her, they gain nothing but a powerful enemy—two, if you count Helena Hu."

Grace threw her hands up into the air. "You're delusional. We have to go to the cops. *Someone* has to be responsible."

Delgado reached toward Grace as if to take hold of her arm but stopped, maybe realizing that doing so would be a very bad idea. "If you go to the police now, you are signing her death warrant. Not to mention my son's. Give me a chance to handle this my way."

I was only a little surprised that Manuel Delgado would go as far as to beg me and Grace when it came to protecting his family. In some ways it might have been honorable, if it didn't involve covering up several murders and leaving a woman at the mercy of the Russian mafia.

"They're going to kill her either way," I told him as firmly as I could. "And I trust the police's chances of finding her way more than I trust yours."

"No, I have a plan. Once we have the money together Sergio and I are going to prove to them that we have the money, and as soon as they release Christine, we will tell them where the money is."

I didn't have to look at Grace to know she'd just rolled her eyes. I could practically hear the sound of it when she spoke. "That just sounds like a plan from a badly written mob movie."

"What if I confess to everything when it's over?" Delgado was without a doubt desperate now. "Christine, the laundering, the dead employee, Carrie, the Russians, everything."

I crossed my arms over my chest. "Those are just words. You can say that now, but as soon as you get your way, it will be like the conversation never happened."

"I'll put it in writing!"

Now there was an interesting idea, and I had to admit it gave me pause. Having Delgado's signed confession would be extremely useful. We could finally get justice for Carrie and whoever else might have been hurt by this man.

But it wouldn't be justice if Manuel Delgado took the blame for his son's actions. So in the end, no matter how tempting that bargain was, it wasn't a deal I was willing to make there with him.

"This is a matter for the police to figure out."

Delgado took several deep breaths, regaining some of his old composure. With a cool voice he said, "You don't work for the police. You work for Helena Hu and you have an obligation to complete the job she's given you in the manner that would best serve your client—that is, her."

I chuckled humorlessly. "Oh, I think Helena Hu would be very well served by seeing you rot in prison."

"Even more so than if you got her daughter back?"

"I think we can manage both."

Delgado returned to his seat behind his desk. "Do you think so? If the Russians get even a whiff of law enforcement, they'll kill her without hesitation, as you've no doubt considered. Your chances are higher with me. Something to think about."

Grace looked at me, and I didn't much care for the expression on her face. "What if he is right about that, Gabe?"

I stepped closer to her, lowering my voice in the hopes Delgado wouldn't overhear us disagreeing. Based on the smug look on his face, that idea was shot to the wind, though.

"Are you kidding me? You don't believe that, do you? There's no way they'll go for the 'let the girl go and we'll give you the money' line!"

"Maybe not, but if they don't then we can bring the FBI in. They'll keep her alive as long as they can because they want their money. They wouldn't have gone through all of this effort otherwise. If this doesn't work, we have the police as a backup plan. But if things get botched with the police, we've lost our chance to bring her back alive."

"This is a terrible idea," I hissed. It wasn't ever wise to make a deal with men like Manuel Delgado. Grace knew that, or at least should have.

"We can at least run it by Helena. She should have a say in this."

"I can't believe you're actually suggesting we don't go to the police with this, Grace."

"I'm not suggesting we don't go. I'm suggesting we give Helena Hu a chance to make a decision that involves her daughter."

"Not going to the police is wrong, and you know it!"

"This isn't about us, Gabe! We're employees. We have a job. I agree with you, and for all I know Helena will agree with you, too. But she should be the one to make that call."

"Fine," I huffed, annoyed. "We can go pay Helena Hu a visit today, and she can decide."

Delgado actually had the balls to grin at us then. "Let me know what she decides."

I turned the full force of my scowl on him. "Don't worry, you'll know when the police come breaking down your door. Come on, Grace, we're done here."

Grace waited until we were in the elevator to speak. "As much as I hate to admit it, he might be our best chance to find Christine."

"Better than the police?"

Grace spread her hands in a *who knows*? gesture. "It might take the police days or weeks to get the information they need to find her. Arresting Delgado isn't going to happen quietly, either. There's no chance it won't hit the news, and when the mafia sees it and suspects why, these men will probably kill Christine. Can we agree on that much?"

"I guess," I allowed, not willing to entirely concede this point to her. "But Grace, a decision like this could blow up in our faces."

The elevator reached the lobby, and as the doors opened, we were met with the dagger-like glare of the woman we'd barreled past on the way in. She said nothing, though, as we left.

The rain had stopped while we were inside. When we left the building, I noticed a man in a suit fall into step behind us, making his way toward the parking lot, as well. He gave off a different vibe than the two Russians, but he still made me uneasy. I was really happy when we finally approached my car. The man, however, was parked next to us, and sped up to walk alongside us.

"Listen closely," he said, voice low, discreet. Grace and I stopped dead in our tracks; my heart raced in my chest. "No, don't stop. Keep walking. There's a flyer on your windshield, an advertisement of some sort. Ignore what it's for; it doesn't matter. Look at the back. You'll find a restaurant's name and address written on it. You need to leave here and go right to that location. Do not make any other stops. I'll be behind you."

I struggled to find words, only half-garbled sounds coming out before I managed, "Who are you?"

Discreetly he adjusted his suit coat, opening it a bit. The first thing my eyes went to was a gun—a big thing, bigger than what Maka used. The second thing I noticed was a set of FBI credentials.

We were now dealing with the Feds.

"WE HAVEN'T DONE anything wrong, right?" Grace asked me for the fourth time as we made our way to the restaurant on the flyer. It was some family chain places guaranteed to be crowded.

"We failed to report a crime. That's probably bad," I said, not really feeling up to comforting her. I kept glancing in the rearview mirror at the man—the FBI agent—who was now following us.

"Yeah, but if they were going to arrest us, they would have done it, right? Not invited us to a family restaurant."

She had a point, but I didn't say so.

It was just before five, and the parking lot of the restaurant was a little over half full, early bird diners getting their dinners out of the way. I pulled into the first open space I could find, the agent taking the one directly next to me, as I expected.

I thought about Maka and how this was going to be a massive chance for him to say I told you so. Also a pretty massive reason for him to express concern over my job.

We entered the restaurant, the FBI agent behind us. The hostess started toward us, but the FBI agent waved her away. He slipped past us, taking the lead and guiding us to a table in the back where a woman in a pantsuit sat, nursing a cup of coffee.

She cast an appraising eye over us, like she was judging us. "So this is them."

"It is," her companion answered, even though it clearly wasn't meant as a question. He motioned us into the chairs across from her and took the one beside her.

"We'll keep this short and to the point," the woman said, taking charge of the conversation immediately. There was a commanding tone to her voice. This was a woman who was no doubt used to working in the hypermasculine world of the FBI. "I'm Special Agent in Charge Proctor, this is Supervisory Special Agent Dallas. We're with the FBI's Organized Crime Unit."

"So this is about the Russians," I confirmed, stomach tightening with nerves.

"It is. We've been working for nearly two years to bring them down. They've been really careful so far. We've spent the last several months focusing our attention on their connection to the Delgados, but have had a hard time getting evidence. That is, until the Russians kidnapped Christine Hu."

The waitress brought Dallas, Grace, and me water, so the conversation fell silent. I glanced around the room, thinking about what Delgado said about the Russians killing Christine if they caught a whiff of police involvement. What if those men were still following us? If they saw us in this meeting, then…

"They're not here," Agent in Charge Proctor assured me, like she could read my mind. "We've got people all around to ensure they didn't follow you."

Grace leaned forward, clasping her hands together on the table in front of her. "What I don't understand is why you haven't done anything to bring Christine home if you've known all along that she's been taken."

"We're trying to bring her back while also bringing the organization and those associated with it down," Dallas said stiffly. "If we act too soon, we could risk twenty months of hard work and kill any chance of success."

Grace looked at him distastefully. "So the Russians are more important to you than a woman's life."

"Don't be so short-sighted," Dallas said scathingly. "How many people like Christine do you think these men have hurt? Or will hurt in the future? Of course we want to see Christine Hu home safely, but we're not going to willingly endanger other people to do it."

"What does any of this have to do with us?" I asked before Grace could piss off a federal agent.

"Like I said, we've turned our attention to Delgado as the weak link, our way to get the Russians," Proctor said, giving Dallas a look I couldn't read. "Delgado is extremely distrustful, though. It's been impossible to get anyone on the inside. We need someone already there. That's where you come in."

"You think Delgado trusts *us*?" Grace laughed. "I'm pretty sure we're his least favorite people in the world, Agent Proctor."

While I agreed with Grace on that, I said, "Well, given what happened today…"

"Is this about the meeting you had with Delgado?"

"It wasn't really a meeting, it was more of a confrontation," I said. Proctor and Dallas listened while Grace and I filled them in on what went down in Delgado's office.

By the time we finished, Proctor had a satisfied smile on her face. "I knew the two of you would be useful. Delgado's desperate. He'll trust you out of necessity."

"I don't know if I like this," I said, though I actually did know, and I *didn't* like it. It seemed far too risky.

"We don't need anything from you but where to make the bust," Proctor said, probably meaning for it to sound comforting. "Our own sources have told us that Delgado has been gathering the money to pay the Russians, and you've verified that. There will be a drop point or a trade-off to get the money to them. We just need to know where that is to catch them."

I was not convinced. "Do you think Delgado is going to believe that we're interested in helping him at this point?"

Agent Proctor arched an eyebrow. "I'm sure you'll be convincing."

"We can just tell him that he was right and Helena wanted to get Christine back and wants us to try it his way," Grace said. "He's such an arrogant prick he wouldn't even think to question that."

I couldn't argue with her on that point. "I'm still not very comfortable with this."

Grace put her hand on my forearm. "You said you wanted to go to the police. Well, this is what they're telling us is best. Maybe we should give it a shot."

I let out a groan and Grace visibly relaxed; she knew it meant I was giving in. "Okay, what do we need to do?"

Chapter Fourteen

I FELT UNEASY about the entire situation when I returned to my condo. Night had fallen and the air had cooled considerably, giving it a pleasant feel. Lights were on in my front window, I noticed from my car. Any wariness I felt was immediately offset by the smell of cooking food coming from inside. I doubted the Russians would break into my apartment to make me dinner.

This was one of the many times that I reminded myself that I really didn't deserve Maka.

The smell intensified when I entered the condo, a mix of sweetness and spice that had my mouth watering. Maka was making hot wings. My appreciation of him was growing steadily by the minute.

"There you are," Maka said in greeting, busy putting a plateful of cooked chicken wings into his personal homemade hot sauce. He wouldn't tell me what was in it, wouldn't even let me be in the room when he made it. It didn't bother me that much—I just enjoyed eating it, I didn't care what he put in it. I made a big deal about it to make him happy. "I was wondering when you were going to get back."

I gestured at the mess that my kitchen had become. "You don't seem all that worried."

"I told the guys on duty when I left to let me know if a cute *haole* ended up dead."

"I'm glad they know I'm cute. Dinner ready?"

"Just got to mix the salad. You mind?"

"Not at all." It felt good to have a task to distract myself, something to keep my focus off the next day when I would be helping in an FBI sting.

My life is way *too interesting.*

I got the mixed salad bag from the crisper and emptied it into a large bamboo bowl. I made a second trip to the fridge and brought out the bottle of sesame dressing that Maka loved.

I managed to make it through dinner without getting too stressed and without talking about my day, asking him about his own instead, which took us full through the meal. It wasn't until I was washing dishes that he finally asked the question.

"How did violating a restraining order go?"

"Can I finish with the dishes before we get into that?"

Maka stopped midway through putting the pan away in its place, turning to look at me. "I don't like the sound of that."

You'll like it even less when I tell you.

Part of me wanted to take my time with the dishes to put off telling him, but I knew that Maka would catch on to that, so instead I rushed. The sooner it was done with the better.

We went and sat on the couch when the dishes were done and I walked him through our run-in with Delgado. The more I said, the more worried Maka got, especially when I mentioned the Russians.

"This isn't good, babe. Men like that, they're monsters. They make Ashford look like a schoolyard bully." I grimaced at the mention of the man who'd tried to kill me on three different occasions. I wasn't the first person Ashford had tried to kill, that much I'd seen in his eyes. He'd been frightening, but these men were on a different level.

"It gets better." I filled him in on Delgado's plan and then the FBI.

"This is insane, Gabe! Do you realize just how much danger you're putting yourself in?"

"Well I can't exactly tell the FBI no," I said dryly. "This is our chance to not only save Christine but also finally bring Delgado down."

"I don't see why you're the one who needs to do any of this," Maka cried, standing up.

I kept a firm grip on my emotions. I was going to remain calm and let him be the one who got worked up. A sort of detached part of my brain was able to observe with some amusement the reversal of roles, since I was usually the one to react emotionally.

"I'm just doing my job."

"Did you ever think that maybe you need a new job?"

I was taken aback by the remark. It wasn't like it was the first time he'd said it, but I never thought he was actually serious when he did. "Excuse me?"

"I'm serious! Do you realize the number of times you've been shot at, strangled, kidnapped, assaulted, or marooned at sea? These aren't problems normal people face in their jobs!"

"Oh come on," I protested, crossing my arms across my chest. "I've never been marooned at sea."

Maka narrowed his eyes. "Remember Biers?"

"He wasn't going to maroon us—he was going to sink us."

"And that's so much better? Your job is too damn dangerous."

The hypocrisy of the statement broke the restraint I had, and I could no longer hold back. "Oh? If that isn't the machete calling the knife dangerous! Do you realize how dangerous your job is? You're a cop! I worry about you all the time when you're on duty!"

"That's different!"

I closed the distance between us until we were standing toe to toe. "How?"

"Because I'm trained for it! I am prepared for the things that come up on the job. You're not! Do you have any idea how fucking difficult it is to watch the man you love go careening through these wild, dangerous situations like he doesn't care what happens to him?"

Maka's words washed over me and I knew I had a dumbfounded expression on my face. Maka saw it, and his expression changed. "What?"

"The man you love?"

Maka tilted his head a little, like he was surprised that part stuck out to me. "Well, yeah. Call me crazy, but yeah."

I blinked, trying to get my thoughts to clear up so I could formulate some sort of response. The word *love* kept bouncing around my head, growing louder and louder, drowning out any other thoughts.

"What? Why are you staring at me? How long can you go without blinking?"

"You've never said that before. That you—that you love me." My heart thumped louder in my chest, so loud I thought it might burst right out.

I wasn't very familiar with the words in my life, beyond the friendly way Grace and I said it to each other. Trevor wasn't capable of love; I'd realized too late. Even if he'd said it, it never would have rung true. I'd never heard my parents use the word, either with me or with each other, not once as far back as I could remember. Maybe that explained why I wasn't so surprised by my parents' divorce.

All in all, this was a pretty big deal for me. Besides, wasn't that a big deal for any couple?

Maka grinned ruefully. "I admit it's not how I imagined saying it for the first time, but there it is. I love you, Gabe Maxfield. I've known it for a while, too. I just didn't want to say it yet, not until I was sure that you felt the same. I told you before that I'm looking for something serious, and now you know how serious I am."

He looked at me then like he was afraid of how I would react, afraid I would think he was coming on too strong or too soon.

In reality I couldn't have been happier to hear those words. My own feelings were quite clear to me: I'd never met someone like Maka, and I'd be an idiot not to love him. He treated me in a way no one else ever had, like I was the most important thing in the world. He was kind, compassionate, charming, and fiercely protective.

I reached out, taking his hands and pulling him against me, my arms circling his waist. I peered up into his eyes. "I love you, too, Maka Kekoa. I came here in a very dark time and you took my hand and pulled me out into the sunshine, both figuratively and literally. I don't know where I would be without you."

"You'd be just fine, because you're an awesome person, and that's about you, not me."

I rose onto my tip toes to kiss him, and it was tender and incredible. A warmth suffused my body and took root in my stomach, a feeling entirely different from arousal. It took me a moment to be able to place it.

Happiness. That's what it was, pure and simple.

"I like what I'm seeing on your face right now," Maka said, voice low. "It's a good look on you."

I smiled, thinking about how I probably looked like Bashful from *Snow White and the Seven Dwarves*. "Do you want to see how well it looks on me in other lighting? Maybe in the bedroom?"

Maka kissed me again. "Okay, I can take a hint. Let's go. After a shower."

THE NEXT MORNING seemed to pass by in fits and spurts, and I was unable to really remember much of any of it. Maka and I had breakfast, but I couldn't tell you ten minutes after what it was that we ate.

Before I knew it, I was at work with Grace and we were waiting for the FBI agents to show up. We'd called Mrs. Neidermeyer and asked her not to come in today, deciding it was best for everyone involved if she wasn't there. We didn't want to put her in unnecessary danger, and we could do without the inevitable distraction she would bring with her.

"They should be here soon, don't you think?" Grace gazed out the door to the parking lot, like she was on high alert, even though they never told us when they would be coming.

"Calm down, you're going to give yourself a heart attack. Just come sit down."

Grace did as I said, but was seated for less than a full minute before she was on her feet and at the door again.

"You know, if the Russians *are* watching us, you're just going to give away that there's something going on. Act normal."

"I don't know how you're acting so calmly," she grumbled.

"Blame my upbringing. It's what happens when you grow up in a family where talking about things just doesn't happen. We repressed and repressed. It's a skill you master."

Grace reluctantly sat down on the arm of Mrs. Neidermeyer's chair, keeping most of her weight in her feet so she didn't tip over. "Well, maybe one day you can give a seminar on how to do it."

"I'll teach you my ways, don't worry."

Grace's cell phone rang and I thought it might be the FBI, which I dismissed because neither Grace nor I gave Agents Proctor and Dallas our cell phones; they knew the number to Paradise Investigations, and they knew where to find us.

"It's Jin," Grace said, sounding more nervous about him being on the phone than she'd been about running a sting for the FBI. "Hello? Hey. No, now is fine."

Grace held up a finger to me and slipped back through the door and into her office.

I took advantage of her absence to take several deep breaths. Sure, I was outwardly calm—like I told Grace, I'd mastered the skill of looking like nothing was wrong a long time ago—but inside my nerves were roiling. I couldn't stop thinking about what Maka said about me ending up in danger an inordinate amount of times. He wasn't wrong. Given my history in the short time I'd been in Hawai'i, I could see Maka's concern. The way our luck was going, Grace and I were going to find ourselves kidnapped by Russians.

I reached out and rapped my knuckles on the faux-wooden surface of Mrs. Neidermeyer's desk.

Grace returned and she actually had a smile on her face. "Good news?"

She nodded. "That was Jin."

"I gathered that much when you said 'It's Jin.' What did he want?"

"He invited me out tonight."

"A second date so soon? That's incredible! I knew he wouldn't be able to resist you if you just showed him the *real* you."

"I owe this to you," she said, pulling me into a hug. "Thank you so much!"

"I'm a miracle worker," I said with a grin.

Just after eleven the FBI arrived and we didn't have time to think about anything but what lay before us.

The task they had for us was relatively simple. We would, wearing a wire, be present with Delgado and get the location of the drop point. After that the agents would do their jobs and we would have done our part in bringing down a massive crime organization and Delgado in one swoop.

In the back, free of any windows, Agent Dallas helped me secure a wire in a place it wouldn't be easily detected, while Agent Proctor did that with Grace.

Once finished, there was nothing left to do but go to meet Delgado. I chose to drive because I didn't trust Grace behind the wheel. The moment the FBI had arrived, whatever calm she'd gained from Jin's phone call evaporated and she was a bundle of nerves once more.

I couldn't say I was much better, though.

Cold dread settled in the pit of my stomach as I pulled into a parking space at Delgado's building. It felt like some sort of perverse antithesis to what I'd experienced the night before with Maka.

"We could always go home," Grace said hopefully.

"Not if we want to get Christine back. Actually, that makes me think of something." I picked up my cell phone and dialed Helena Hu's number. I felt like she deserved to know what was going on. I hated thinking of her waiting, unsure, not knowing what was happening with her daughter. We couldn't give her any details, because it was an ongoing investigation now, but we could at least let her know something was happening. If the FBI didn't like it, they could get over it.

"Hello? Mr. Maxfield? Has something happened?"

A sharp stab of guilt went through me, then, at the near-frantic tone in her voice. "No, nothing's happened, Mrs. Hu. I'm sorry to just call out of nowhere, but I felt like we needed to let you know. There's not any details we can give you—and I'm honestly sorry about that, but we can't. I hope you can trust us—but we *can* tell you that we're going to do our best to reunite you with Christine today."

There was a stunned silence that seemed to tick by forever before she finally spoke. "What are you talking about?"

"Like I said, I can't give you details. I just wanted to let you know. One of us will call you as soon as we can." I hung up before she could ask me more questions, because not being able to answer them was driving me crazy.

"That was a good thing you did," Grace said, reaching out and squeezing my hands. We remained like that for maybe half a minute, just drawing strength from each other. I was able to take comfort in knowing that the FBI was listening from wherever it was they'd set up their command post. If shit hit the fan, ideally they'd be able to come running.

Or they'd leave us there to rot and not risk blowing their operation; it was hard to tell.

"Okay, let's go."

Leaving the car, I did my best to put on a confident face, hoping that Delgado couldn't look at my face and know exactly what we were up to. A quick glance at Grace surprised me. She'd managed to slip on this fierce, confident mask. She reminded me of Agent Proctor—strong, powerful, and in control. I was glad to be walking in next to her.

We were greeted in the front lobby by Delgado's personal assistant. She looked like we were the last people in the world she wanted to see, and she didn't even attempt to hide it.

Her lip curled up before she spoke. "Come with me."

Delgado was behind his desk when we entered, a glass of what looked like scotch in his hand. For the first time, he looked disheveled, a raw moment where the fierce mask of the millionaire CEO had broken, revealing a troubled man inside. The fact that his troubles were of his own making and the result of his lack of scruples made it impossible for me to feel anything close to sympathy for him.

The personal assistant cleared her throat, and I stepped aside so she could see her boss. "Will you need anything else, Mr. Delgado?"

"I'm fine, thanks. You can go home for the rest of the day."

She opened her mouth like she wanted to argue, her frown deepening. In the end, she surrendered to the will of her boss. "Yes, sir."

The door closed behind us with a loud *click*.

"I'm expecting the call any minute now," he said, staring at the glass in his hand, not looking at us. "They'll call and tell me where the drop is to be made and what time."

"We're looking at a very different Manuel Delgado," I remarked, gesturing up and down at him. "The stress of your crimes finally catching up with you?"

"While you perhaps don't want to believe it, I am merely a man who is doing his best to protect his family. I would think you would do the same."

I snorted. "I'm the wrong man to talk about family with, Mr. Delgado."

Delgado finally looked our way, gesturing toward Grace with the glass he still held in his hand. "Well, think of the lengths you went to for her, Mr. Maxfield. Family isn't always blood."

"On that we agree," I said, patting Grace on her shoulder. "But there some things I wouldn't do, even for her."

"I don't know if that makes you a better or lesser man than I."

I rolled my eyes. "Whatever you have to tell yourself to sleep at night. But if you really think that, then I'm not surprised your son ended up in this situation."

Delgado bristled at my mention of Sergio. Grace, however looked around the office. "Where is your son, by the way? I thought he'd want to be here for such an important moment."

"He's making the exchange," Delgado said stiffly. "He wants his face to be the first one Christine sees when she's free."

"He might not be her favorite person," I mused.

"Maybe she'll slap him," Grace suggested.

I had to admit the idea of Sergio's smug face getting slapped was enticing. I almost wished I could be there to see it happen in person. I also found it satisfying that Sergio Delgado himself would be picked up by the FBI in the act. There was no escape.

"When do you think the call is coming?" I asked Delgado, reluctantly taking a seat across from him.

"They didn't exactly give me a schedule, Mr. Maxfield." Delgado rose and refilled his glass.

"Maybe you shouldn't be drinking so early in the day, Manny," Grace chided. "Dulls the senses, you know?"

"Trust me, the alcohol is *helping* me right now. Would you like one?" Grace shook her head. "No? What about you, Mr. Maxfield?"

"No, I'm fine." I didn't want a drink, all I wanted was for this nonsense to be over, Christine to be home and Delgado—both of them—to be in jail. By the end of the day it would happen. Now I just needed to be patient.

"Did you write that statement for us?" I asked Delgado when he returned with his refilled drink.

"I did." Delgado took a tri-folded packet of paper from his desk. "In here you'll find very exact details about everything I told you about already. It's signed, as well." He offered it to me, but I hesitated to take it. "What, decided you don't want this anymore?"

"That depends. Did *you* confess in this, or did you tell the truth?"

"What does it matter, Mr. Maxfield? He's my son. In the end, responsibility falls on my shoulders either way. The choices he made are a result of my upbringing, and I will own that."

Grace shook her head pityingly. "You've learned nothing. The worst thing you can do is take responsibility for your son's choices. He's a grown man, and he made the mistakes. All you are doing is preventing him from growing as a person and from learning that there are consequences for his actions."

"You'll forgive me if I don't rush to take the words of someone who has never been a parent."

The phone on Delgado's office table rang, then, and all three of us froze, our eyes glued to it. This was it, the moment we'd been waiting for. Now that it had actually come, my heart was pounding in my chest. I wondered if the sound of it thumping would in any way impact the wire hidden on my body. I doubted that could happen, though, so I tried not to worry.

I got up and went around the side of the desk to stand next to Delgado, just in case. Grace did the same on his other side as the phone still rang.

"Go on, before they think you backed out," Grace urged when Delgado still hadn't answered it.

Delgado nodded, took one last drink, and then answered the phone. "Manuel Delgado. Yes... Yes, I have the money. All of it, and it's ready to be taken to you. Yes, I remember the rules. Sergio will bring it to you alone. In ten minutes? Where?" Delgado listened and then rattled off an address that I didn't recognize, writing it down on a scrap piece of paper as he did.

I hoped that the FBI was copying it down, as well. Considering it was the FBI, I imagined they'd relayed the address and were already en route at that moment.

"He'll be there. Make sure she's there as well. If you cross me, I will make you regret it."

Delgado hung up the phone and looked between Grace and I. "It's done. Now all that's left is to tell Sergio."

Grace came back around his desk to stand beside me as Delgado picked up the phone to call his son. "I don't know why, but I'm getting a bad feeling here."

I looked at her skeptically. "Why? Because things are actually going smoothly for us? No, wait, I totally get your point. I think it's just paranoia, though."

Delgado held the phone to his ear, drumming his index finger on his desk, some sort of nervous action. "They're ready to make the trade. Be careful."

That was it. The phone call ended as quickly as it had begun. Something about it set strangely with me, like something was off, but I couldn't immediately put my finger on it.

Grace, however, had no problem. "You didn't tell him where the drop is taking place."

Delgado raised an eyebrow. "Oh?"

And I understood. "When did you know?"

"The mafia isn't the only one that has eyes and ears all over," Delgado said, sounding as patronizing as ever. Was this image he'd presented, the shaken father staring defeat in the face, a sham? It seemed like he'd acted that way to lower our defenses, and unfortunately I think it worked.

"They're listening right now," I said, hoping to shake him.

Delgado smirked, showing me that it didn't work. "I doubt it. The moment they heard where the meeting was taking place they took off. They went com silent, no doubt. They won't realize until they get there, and by then it will be too late."

"Was that phone call even about the drop?"

Delgado shook his head. "No, it wasn't. That was my maid at home, right on schedule. I hope you didn't honestly expect me to throw my son under the bus."

"What do you think is going to happen when Christine is free? She's going to turn him in."

Delgado waved a hand dismissively. "Sergio will be her hero, Mr. Maxfield. She will be far too grateful for his coming to her rescue to think about why she's there. Love overlooks a multitude of sins."

I wanted to tell him he was wrong, but thinking about Trevor, I really couldn't. Instead I asked, "Where is the exchange happening?"

"Do you really think that I'm going to just break down and tell you that easily? I'm doing what I must to protect my family."

I turned, exasperated, to Grace. "I can't believe we let this—what?" She had this look on her face that didn't seem appropriate. "What are you thinking?"

"I'm thinking Delgado doesn't have to tell us. I'm pretty sure I know *exactly* where the trade is going down."

Chapter Fifteen

GRACE AND I made a hurried exit from the building. I half expected Delgado to call security to stop us, but he didn't. Perhaps he thought Grace would be wrong in her deduction. He didn't know her like I did, though, and the confidence she stated it with made it plain to me that she did know, or else very much believed she did.

"Okay, where are we going?" I asked when we were in the lobby.

"We're going to—Maka!" Grace stopped cold, staring in surprise. I hadn't even noticed my boyfriend standing there in the lobby until she said his name, I was so wrapped up in figuring out what was going on.

"What are you doing here?" I asked suspiciously.

"I figured the two of you were going to end up doing something stupid, so I wanted to be nearby just in case."

"Well," I said, resuming my walk, "you're in luck. We're going to do something stupid right now."

Maka sighed. "Wonderful. Where are we going?"

"Dostavka," Grace answered, and I realized how obvious it was. No idea how I hadn't made the connection myself. But I often said Grace was smarter than me, and she proved it again and again.

Maka slowed for a moment. "Am I supposed to know where that is?"

"I'll guide you," I said, grabbing his hand and hurrying him along.

Maka drove, speeding along the road, though he didn't use his police siren because he didn't want to spook the mafia or Sergio and put Christine in danger.

As we drove, I called Agent Proctor. She didn't answer, so I left a voicemail, giving her the address for Dostavka and urging her to get there as soon as she could. Hopefully Maka, Grace, and I would be enough until then.

Maka guided his car into a parking lot a block away from Dostavka so our approach wouldn't be noticed right away. Grace started to open her door, but Maka locked them and rounded on us before we could, making sure we were both looking at him.

"Don't do anything stupid, do you understand? Let me take the lead on this one. If anything happens, you two need to get out of there. Agreed?"

Grace and I nodded and chorused, "Agreed."

Maka took his gun from the glove compartment, securing it at his hip before taking his badge, which he kept on a chain, and hanging it around his neck. "Let's go."

I was more than happy to let Maka take the lead on this. I didn't like the idea of him going into what could be a really messy situation with just his gun and badge, but his arguments the night before made sense; he *was* trained to handle situations like this, where Grace and I were not. I had to trust him.

An expensive-looking Hummer was parked just outside of Dostavka and the gate was wide open. Looked like Grace's instincts on this one were right.

We went inside the gate, but there was no noise, no sign that anything had taken place yet. Unless we were too late. We rounded the corner and found Sergio standing there, looking anxious, a briefcase in his hand. His eyes widened, his mouth dropping open when he saw us.

"What—how? No, you can't be here. You have to leave. If they find you here—"

"They haven't come yet?" Maka asked, voice all-business. "How soon before they get here?"

"It could be any second now," Sergio said, voice verging on panicked. "If they find you here, they're going to kill her—hell, all of us. You can't be here."

"We need you to know that we're not going to let them or you walk out of here," Maka said.

"I don't care what happens to me, damn it! I just want Christine free."

This was a man who was lost, I realized, studying him. He'd made some terrible choices in his life, and he was facing the consequences. The world had caught up with him, and he'd never found himself in a situation like this before. His father certainly hadn't done him any favors.

"I think he's right," Grace said. "We need to get out of sight until Christine is free, at least."

Maka thought it over for a minute before nodding. "Fine. We'll get out of sight over there." Maka gestured toward a stack of pallets three stacks across and two stacks high, some place halfway between the gate and where Sergio stood.

"Shit," Sergio cried suddenly, and for a moment I couldn't figure out why, but then I caught it—a low buzzing sound that I couldn't place.

"What? What is that?"

"It's a motorboat," Maka answered.

Sergio gulped almost audibly. "It's them. Go, quickly."

The three of us scurried across the space, ducking behind the pallets. Luckily there was some space between the stacked pallets, and we had a limited view of the scene.

Sergio stood there, his weight shifting from foot to foot as a motorboat drew up to the space. I caught sight of three men on it. I was pretty sure that one of them was Ponytail, but I couldn't be sure.

"Do either of you see Christine?" Grace whispered, trying to find an angle that gave her a good look.

"She's being taken out of the boat now," Maka said, apparently able to see her from his standpoint.

From my space I could see Sergio. One of the three men joined Sergio. A conversation took place between them, though we were too far away to hear it.

I saw the briefcase pass from Sergio to whoever this third man was—he was big and bulky, his head bald and shiny in the afternoon sun.

"There she is!" I gasped as Christine came into sight. She looked a little worse for wear, but unharmed. All I could think was thank god she was alive. The trade done, Sergio took a clearly shaken Christine by the hand, pulling her in close to him and turning on his heel, hustling her away, looking back over his shoulder every now and then.

"Fuck," Maka murmured, and he drew his gun from his belt. I couldn't see what he saw, so I had no idea what it was he was reacting to, but I guessed that it wasn't good.

Sergio and Christine had just gone past the pallets where we hid when a voice called out across the space.

"Delgado!"

Sergio turned. Something he saw made his eyes widen, and he shoved Christine to the ground.

At the same time, Maka stepped out from where he was concealed, gun drawn. "Drop your weapons!" His voice was booming, brooked no arguments.

A gunshot rang out, and I yelped. My first thought was that Maka had been shot. It took my brain a moment to process that it was Sergio who'd crumpled to the ground, not Maka.

Another gunshot split the air, this one closer—Maka returning fire before he ducked back behind the pallets, crouching low.

I realized Christine was still out there in the open and in danger. I didn't think; I just darted out from the relative safety of the pallets and sprinted, crouched low, to where Christine was.

"Come on," I urged, taking her hand.

"Who are you?" Christine cried.

Maka, who'd just darted out to return fire, was caught off guard by my movement. He glanced toward me, anger clear on his face. "Gabe, what the hell are you doing?"

Another shot rang out and Christine screamed next to me. Not far from where we stood the ground cracked from the impact of the bullet and Maka ducked back into cover.

By some miracle Christine and I made it back behind the pallets. "Are you okay?" I asked, looking her over.

"I'm fine, I think."

"Uh, Gabe?"

The panic in Grace's voice made me turn. She was crouched next to Maka, who'd slid down to sit on the ground, back against the pallets, hands pressed against his abdomen. It was impossible for me to miss the stark color of blood as it seeped from between his fingers and around his palms, staining his shirt.

"Oh my god. Oh my god!"

I scurried to him, studying his face, trying to get an idea how bad it was. Of course it was bad—he was shot, for fuck's sake. His eyes were squeezed shut and his teeth were clenched, lips pulled back into a grimace.

"This isn't good," Grace said. "What are we going to do, Gabe?"

I thrust my phone into Grace's hands, nearly dropping it. "Call 911. Quickly. Make sure you tell them officer down."

"I'm okay," Maka hissed.

"You're not okay, you were shot!"

Please, please let him be okay. I can't lose him. A primal fear unlike anything I had ever felt before clawed at me, threatening to steal the breath from my lungs, the strength from my body. I feared that any minute I would black out from oxygen deprivation, but I didn't seem capable of forcing my lungs to work.

The pallets above our heads exploded into a thousand tiny pieces then as more gunfire struck them. Maka was shot, and we were still in deep shit. This wasn't going to end well.

Beside me Grace was still on the phone with the 911 operator, stressing that an officer had been shot, when the sound of sirens filled the air.

"That was fast," I said, relieved.

"I only just told them where we are," Grace said, confused.

The siren grew to an ear-splitting level as a black SUV with a blue light in the windshield came speeding into the property, not stopping at the gate.

From that point on, everything went far too fast for me to remember, as focused as I was on Maka. The Russians were taken down and Christine was hustled off to one of the SUVs. Agents Proctor and Dallas tried to get what happened out of Grace and me, though she provided most of the answers.

My focus stayed on Maka. He was clearly in pain, but he remained conscious. I leaned my forehead against his, doing everything in my power to keep the tears from flowing.

After what felt like an eternity, the ambulances arrived. Paramedics loaded Sergio into one and Maka into the other. They were kind enough to let me ride in the back with him. As they closed us in the metal contraption and began their examination of his wound, I clenched my eyes closed and said a genuine prayer for the first time in a very long time.

THE KNOCK ON the hospital room door startled me from awake. I'd been dozing in the chair next to Maka's hospital bed. The room had become my de facto home; I hadn't left it in the thirty hours Maka had been admitted except when they forced me to overnight. But even then, I just went and slept in the nearby waiting room.

Maka was resting peacefully in the bed, hooked up to an IV.

Grace and Jin stood in the door. "Hey. Sorry we didn't get here earlier. It's been a nightmare of paperwork with the FBI and wrapping things up with Helena." I stood up and Grace hurried to me, pulling me into a tight hug, as if in doing so she could transfer some of her own strength to me. "How is he?"

"I'm fine," Maka answered, eyes still closed.

"You should be resting," I chided as he struggled into a sitting position.

"Like I said, I'm fine. The doctor said the bullet only tore through muscle and fat."

"How'd you get that lucky?" Jin asked, reaching out to take my hand in what I thought would be a handshake but ended in him pulling me into a tight hug too.

"He was turning to look at me," I replied against Jin's shoulder. "Lucky thing, too. He turned at just the right time. If he hadn't, it would have been worse."

"If I hadn't looked at you, I wouldn't have gotten shot," Maka reminded me unnecessarily.

"Let's not play the blame game here." I returned to the chair, lowering myself slowly; the long time spent in it had played hell on my back. "Anyway, he's going to be okay, but he's going to need about six weeks to recover, at the earliest, and isn't going to be doing anything strenuous for the time being. How is everything out there?"

"Sergio came through his surgery. they think he's going to recover. The Russians have scattered to the wind, so Agent Proctor isn't so happy about that." Grace sat down on the edge of the chair, rubbing my head as if I were a little kid. "Christine immediately called off the engagement to Sergio, and she can identify several prominent members of the Russian mafia, which lessened Proctor's displeasure."

"She didn't tell you the worst part," Jin said, ignoring the glare she sent his way. "Didn't want to give you bad news while you were here. I think you'd rather hear it from us."

"Later, Jin," Grace said firmly.

"No, might as well do it now," Maka said wearily. "I'm on a lot of painkillers."

"As soon as he recovers, Sergio is going into Witness Protection."

I swore loudly. "Are you kidding me?"

"He has enough information from his dealings with the Russians to be useful to the FBI. They're putting him in the program in exchange for his cooperation and testimony. Manuel Delgado also came out of this scot-free. Got immunity in exchange for his testimony against the Russians they could catch."

I slumped back in the chair, shaking Grace's hand away. "Of course he did."

"There is a bright side to that," Grace said with a wicked grin. "Delgado's company stock plummeted. Rumor has it the Board of Directors is calling for a vote of no confidence to remove him from the company."

"Okay, that does make me feel better."

"Oh, that paparazzo keeps calling. We owe him that exclusive story, remember?"

I sighed. "Fine. A phone interview, that's it. And no pictures."

They stayed and chatted with Maka and me for about twenty minutes, until it finally looked like Maka was back asleep. At that point I walked them to the door.

"Oh, Gabe, your parents have called the office a few times," Grace said, stopping at the door. "Do you want me to...?"

I shook my head. "No, I'll give them a call. I told them I'd try to see them one more time before they left the island. Maybe I'll get them to come by the hospital and meet them in the waiting room or something."

Grace looked at me with the strangest smile on her face. "You know, I'm really impressed by the way you're handling them."

I shrugged. "There's nothing to be impressed about. For all I know they've assuaged their consciences and when they fly out of here it'll be the last time I ever see them, and that's fine. If something does progress from here, well then, I guess it's a start. I don't know how much I think people can change."

"They can," Grace said confidently. "You did." She pulled me in for one more hug. "I need to get going. Jin and I are going to watch movies at his place. Call me if you need anything."

I waited until Grace rounded the corner at the end of the hallway before I went back inside to my uncomfortable chair. The sound of Maka breathing was soothing, especially since there had been a long time, when he was in surgery, that I didn't know whether or not I was going to hear him breathe again.

I pulled my cell phone out of my pocket and looked at it indecisively. Well, maybe people could change, and maybe Grace was right about me changing, too.

Watching Maka's chest rise and fall, I dialed my mother's hotel room number.

About the Author

J. C. Long is an American expat living in Japan, though he's also lived stints in Seoul, South Korea—no, he's not an army brat; he's an English teacher. He is also quite passionate about Welsh corgis and is convinced that anyone who does not like them is evil incarnate. His dramatic streak comes from his lifelong involvement in theatre. After living in several countries aside from the United States, J. C. is convinced that love is love, no matter where you are, and he is determined to write stories that demonstrate exactly that. J. C. Long's favorite things in the world are pictures of corgis, writing, and Korean food (not in that order...okay, in that order). J. C. spends his time when not writing by thinking about writing, coming up with new characters, attending Big Bang concerts, and wishing he was writing. The best way to get him to write faster is to motivate him with corgi pictures. Yes, that is a veiled hint.

Email: jclongauthor@gmail.com

Facebook: www.facebook.com/authorjclong

Twitter: j_c_long_author

Website: www.jclongauthor.wixsite.com/home

Other books by this author

New Year's Eve Unzipped
Unzipping 7D

A Matter of Duty
A Matter of Courage
A Matter of Justice

Mai Tais and Murder
Hula Dancers and Hauntings
Tiki Torches and Treasures

On Andross Station

Also Available from NineStar Press

Connect with NineStar Press

Website: NineStarPress.com

Facebook: NineStarPress

Facebook Reader Group: NineStarNiche

Twitter: @ninestarpress

Tumblr: NineStarPress